orange

A LuvByte Novella

dawn lanuza

Orange

Dawn Lanuza

Contact the author: hello@dawnlanuza.com

Cover design by Reginald Lapid (https://www.redbubble.com/people/rwowl/shop)

Illustration by Melon Illustration (https://www.instagram.com/mel0nillustrati0n)

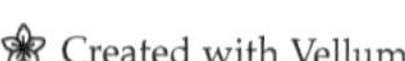 Created with Vellum

she just wanted to sleep. he just wanted to sing. couldn't they just call it quits?

Being woken up by a loud singing voice was not how Yasmin envisioned her Sunday morning, especially after her night shift. Unfortunately, she lived in an apartment above the popular boy group, LuvByte.

Being reported for "noise" is not what Kota would call his well-managed, money-making, life-changing singing voice. Too bad his neighbor and her cat hated his guts.

He's annoying. She's intimidating. Yet they can't seem to help but run into each other…

content note

ORANGE IS HEAT LEVEL 3. This book follows the #RomanceClass guidelines requiring HEA / HFN for romance.

Heat levels are about sex content and as follows:

0 – No sex on or off the page

1 – Off-page sex mentioned in story

2 – At least one "Closed door" sex scene

3 – At least one "Open door" sex scene

4 – Explicit erotic romance with HEA / HFN*

Heat level 4 description mentions HEA/HFN because the acts might include someone who isn't part of the pairing.

one

. . .

I HATE HIM, *I hate him, I hate him.*

Yasmin focused on the numbers in the elevator, grinding her teeth as she tried to be on the farthest side of the cube.

All she could see was the back of his head, where a stupid mole was right on the side of his nape. He wasn't that tall, thank God. She was just an arm reach's away from pulling his hair in case he ever said anything, or breathed too loud.

He was on the other side, diagonal to where she was standing, unable to skip the elevator ride after he made a big deal of shouting, "Wait!" His bony hands stopped the elevator from fully closing.

She saw the regret on his face when he realized that it was her in the elevator but he didn't have the decency to let her take this one alone.

I hate him, I hate him, I hate him.

Finally, the elevator door opened.

You better not turn your head. Not even an inch. A centimeter. Don't you dare glance at me. The look he gave her earlier was enough. If there was anything she learned about this guy, it was this: he was too damn obvious. When he's mad, the tip of his ears gets red, his mouth purses, and he starts to look like a little hamster.

At last, he left. He went straight out of the elevator without looking back. *Good.*

A small laugh escaped from her mouth. She had been so tense inside the box that she must have held her breath the entire time.

Her ride was short for she was, unfortunately, living just a floor above his unit. The first time she met him was not so long ago but it was the worst.

There was a question on Family Feud about what occupation makes one a bad neighbor, and the contestants mentioned drug dealers and the like.

Yasmin had one answer to this question: singers.

Can't even catch a break, Kota closed his door—even the double lock—and exhaled. He held his breath inside the elevator because elevators always made him feel weird, but today, he had to deal with the fact that he had to share it with *her*.

Her, because he never knew her name, even after that time he had to sit through her red-faced, messy hair, teary-eyed yelling at the office of the Home Associations Board.

Life was quiet in Roman's Court before she moved in three months ago. He had been living here with the rest of the LuvByte boys for four years, and people knew who they were, and didn't seem to have a problem with them. Nobody complained, even if he knew that they had trouble keeping the house quiet at all times. There were seven boys in one apartment unit, and there would be running, yelling, laughing, and obnoxious singing sometimes. He was always apologetic about it the following morning and made sure he did a nice thing to make up for it. The neighbors would be forgiving and give them a hearty chuckle.

But *she* was the first one to complain.

And she took it directly to the President of HAB, before 8 in the morning, on a Sunday.

It was the kind of chaos she brought when she moved in, along with her menace of a cat who kinda looked like her: black with smooth fur and gorgeous green eyes. It hissed at him that one time he tried to say hi.

She probably taught that cat to hate him. Except…her cat had the strange habit of climbing down from her balcony to theirs, hanging out there for a bit before climbing up again through the trellis. Kota didn't know if she knew this or even cared.

Kota turned and found Oli, their resident songwriter, staring at him, eyes darting from the double lock and to him. "Fans?"

He shook his head, raising one hand to point above the ceiling.

"God?"

He would have laughed at that, except he was still trying to fill his lungs with air he refused to breathe during that excruciating elevator ride.

"Ah," Oli snapped his fingers. "Pardon me. It's the Goddess upstairs."

He let his tongue out as if that alone left a bad taste in his mouth. Ever since that complaint, the boys started calling their upstairs neighbor *Goddess*, after Kota mistakenly used the term to describe her. He said *Goddess of Wrath*, and somehow the only thing they picked up was that he thought that she was a Goddess when—

"More like the devil. A witch." He spat. She had long, straight black hair parted in the middle, and she always looked like she just came back from the beach. She was morena with cheeks looking a bit sunburnt, with a splash of subtle and dainty freckles on the bridge of her nose and cheeks. Her neck was long, and she acted taller than everyone else. She's beautiful—he wasn't blind—but he could never *not* see her as the first time he heard her speak, or cry, for that matter.

"How's that going for you?" Oli asked, pulling him out of his reverie.

"31 days." He answered, annoyed that he had been counting down the days. He had been on probation for 60 days. *Absolutely no singing in the balcony or corridors for 60 days,* which was ridiculous, because whoever said that he was making noise?

If his singing was considered noise, then what does it say about the people who had to pay to hear him sing?

This was his job, singing. He was LuvByte's main vocalist, did she even know that? He was ranked #1 out of all the boys for his vocal prowess after they finished training. He took pride in that because if there was anything that Kota knew at a very young age, it was that he was really, really good at singing.

He could hit notes most people couldn't, and he enjoyed challenging himself into reaching such notes and trained himself for years to manage and take care of his voice. Which meant yes, salabat every morning and no talking for stretches of days for vocal rest. She just happened to catch him pre-concert and Kota liked to practice, even at home.

Nobody complained before.

Nobody.

So to have someone call HAB to report him is just...

He scrunched his nose at the memory of it, still mad at the idea of someone hating his voice so much she would call someone to make him stop. And then made him stop doing it for 60 days.

"You're doing it again." Oli pointed at him.

Kota forgot that Oli was still there. He looked like he probably just woke up, his hair still sticking up in weird places.

Kota straightened his face. "What?"

"Gigil face." He teased. "I told you, just talk to her."

"Me?" He laughed at that suggestion like he did the last time. "And tell her what? Sorry for existing?"

Oli looked so amused; he tipped his cup to suppress a laugh.

"I'm going to my room," he said instead, eager to rest.

"You have a visitor, by the way."

"Hmm?" Kota opened the door to their room. He slept at the top bunk, and *lo and behold*. Sleeping in his bed was the black cat from upstairs.

two

. . .

"YOU CAN HOLD THE CAT HOSTAGE," Chili suggested, scratching the cat's neck.

Kota kept his hand on his hip, watching their youngest member play with the cat. Like its owner, the cat played favorites, and it seemed like Chili was the frontrunner.

"Why would I do that?" he asked. The cat slept in his bed for four hours and moved to the living room while they were eating dinner—which conveniently—had fried fish in it. It had since rubbed their legs and asked for food.

"He's a bargaining chip," Chili answered, then craned his neck to the cat's butt. "Remind me again if you're a boy?"

Kota watched him raise the cat's tail swiftly, then dropped his head. "I'm sorry, little guy. It's probably for the best."

He turned to Kota and mouthed, "Neutered."

"I don't want to keep the cat here."

"Why?" Chili pouted. "He likes it here."

"He's been here for a day, *relax*." Kota rolled his eyes. Pets were something members of their group wanted to get, but with the space they currently have with their erratic schedule, it was just not practical to get one.

Plus, he'd probably end up cleaning after it. He knew

cats would probably be less work than dogs, but this is *not* their cat. This is the devil's cat, and it probably is the devil, too.

"He keeps coming to us," Chili reasoned.

The cat stared at him right then, its green eyes turned into slits as if it knew what he was thinking.

"Go home," he told the cat as if it could understand him.

It blinked at him, then turned away.

"He said no," Chili interpreted.

"You should take him there," Kota recommended, impatient to get this over with. He wanted to sleep when he came home, but with that cat in his bed, he had to settle for the couch. He was *so* tired and needed to sleep more, but he needed to learn this new song he was going to record for a movie.

"Why don't you take him if you're so eager to let him go?"

"Just let him out of the balcony and close the door."

"It's raining!" he complained.

"It'll go home." Kota countered.

"Just take him home, then."

Kota's brows furrowed, aware that their youngest managed to switch the orders. He was clever that way; it was what endeared him to the guy.

"Just take the cat, knock on her door, hand him over, and maybe she'll forgive you for pissing her off that one time."

"I didn't do anything!"

"You were singing the same line for half an hour."

"No," he shook his head. He wouldn't stay in one place for that long. Unless he hasn't perfected it, he would listen to it, then go back, and—"If you think that's annoying, why didn't you say anything?"

"I've lived with you for years. Why do you think I wear earplugs at night?"

"I don't sing at night."

"No, but you like to belt out a high C in the morning."

He wanted to say *no*, but actually, yeah, he does that. It was a good warm-up exercise, a casual run to start his day.

He hadn't been doing that because he had that 60-day notice. He started going to the studio earlier to practice but sometimes, he would go to the Emergency Exit stairway to rehearse. Acoustics were great, and not a lot of people use it. What are the chances she would be there? Close to nothing. So *if* he really needed, he would sometimes pop in there to sing.

So far, no one has reported him.

Chili took the cat and handed it over to him. The cat hissed, and it made him step back.

"It hates me."

"Probably cause you keep calling him *it*." Chili ran a gentle hand over its fur. "I'd like to say that he won't bite but in your case, he probably would."

"If this cat eats me alive," he warned.

"Then you can report them to the HAB. It'd be a fun reunion with the neighbor upstairs."

———

It was all her fault. Yasmin left the balcony door open for a minute, forgetting that Cosmo had been out of his cage since that morning.

She forgot to close it when she left the apartment to get some supplies, and by the time she returned, the cat had already been missing.

She'd been panicking since, looked around the corridors, and asked the guards if they saw her cat walking around the area.

Her next course of action was to print out Cosmo's photos so she can post them around: in the elevator, at the community board—of course, she'd have to ask the home associations board first. She didn't want to post online just yet, just in case she found the cat on the premises, but it was starting to get dark. It had been raining, too, making it harder for her to believe that she was gonna find her cat.

She cried at the thought of her cat lost—her anxiety heightened as she was about to get her period any time this week. She's already gone through the motions: the irritability, the sensitivity to sounds, the crying (again), and the big zit on her forehead saying hello to her this morning.

She'd been texting her friends about it, and Nico, who she used to live with when they were both in nursing school, had volunteered to come over and help her look.

A quick knock on her door made her jump right up, eager to see a friendly face after what was shaping up to be a horrible day.

"Just a sec," she called out, mindlessly fishing for the pair of slippers on the floor. She ran to the door, ready to throw herself into her friend's arms.

It wasn't her friend.

It was *so* not her friend.

It was him, the noisy gargoyle living downstairs with—

"Cosmo!"

The cat practically leaped out of his hands, and she heard him yelp at that. She didn't care though, because Cosmo was here, her beautiful, wonderful, mischievous cat who liked to see her suffer, but she loved him anyway.

The cat ran straight inside their apartment as if it were escaping the man.

As he should, she thought, before turning back to him.

"What did you do to him?" she asked, eyes narrowed.

"What did I do to him?" he repeated. *God, his voice is so loud.* Does this man know that he could speak at a decibel lower? "What did *your* cat do to me?"

He raised his hand and showed a long scratch from Cosmo's claws, the edges starting to swell. Yasmin gasped at the sight of it and grabbed his hand by reflex to examine any wounds.

He was startled but didn't flinch or move from her grasp. She could feel him watching her from her periphery, and it made her step back as she was satisfied.

"No wounds," she announced — although she wasn't sure if it was more for her than him. She had a quick moment of panic. As a healthcare professional, she knew how dangerous cat scratches and bites could be.

He looked at her like she was not making sense, his ears turning pink. Yasmin interpreted this as him getting mad. Or maybe…just concerned.

She took a deep breath. *Alright. Fine.* It seemed to Yasmin that she was standing in the middle of two roads: being an awful, petty person and being a responsible person and pet owner.

She could be petty at any time, but she could never be irresponsible. It's who she *is*. As a working nurse, it's in her blood to help. As a pet owner, she took pride in her pets — even the ones she had back at her parents' house in La Union: a dog named Siga (her dad named him) and another cat named Mingming. They were all healthy, friendly, wonderful pets who never hurt another person.

She pushed her door open. The layout of her apartment showed the kitchen first, so she had a sink close to the door. He was still at the doorway when she glanced, "You have to wash it. Just in case."

She turned the faucet on and beckoned him with her right hand. He stepped in awkwardly but hurried at the sight of the running water.

Yasmin stepped away and ran to her bathroom to get a bar of soap. He turned off the faucet as he waited for her to return and only turned it back on when he was washing the wound.

"Wash it well, okay," she said as she walked over to her closet to get a fresh towel.

He was uncharacteristically quiet. All she heard was the faucet turning off by the time she returned. He had his shirt rolled up, his arm wet and dripping on the sink. He looked contemplative with his other hand resting on the sink.

She handed him the towel, and he took it with thanks. It was the first time she heard his voice at a normal, room-appropriate level, and it was…a nice voice. Why can't he be like this every day?

"Do you need some bandaids?"

He shook his head. "I have them. I think."

She shook her head and started to go through her drawer where the first aid kit was. He was standing awkwardly right by the sink, and if they weren't so estranged, she would have laughed by now and told him to relax.

But he kept his hand on his arm, standing there, just… waiting for her.

She came to him, opening the bandaid.

"There's no wound." He told her this time.

She let her thumb run through the slightly swollen skin, and she felt the intake of his breath like a sharp inhale. She paused and decided to be gentle, putting on a bandaid in the area anyway, and pressing it lightly.

"Cosmo's vaccinated," Yasmin informed him.

"I am, too."

Yasmin tilted her head. "You get bitten by pets a lot?"

He relaxed a bit at that. "My niece got a puppy earlier this year."

She nodded as he lifted his hand, showing her a non-existent scar. It was probably not a deep wound either.

"How's the dog?" She winced the moment she said it. It sounded like she was more concerned with the pet than him.

"I'm still alive, aren't I?" he answered, running a hand through the bandaid she put on. It was a printed one, with cartoon drawings of hearts. "Don't worry, I won't die from this. Masamang damo and all."

She didn't know if she should laugh at that. She didn't know him well enough to know if it was a joke. *Would a bad person joke about being one?* She certainly didn't have the best impression of him when they first met.

He didn't say anything else for a while but cleared his throat to nudge his thumb to the door.

"Sorry about that," she said finally, pointing to his arm.

He just nodded, nonchalant.

Yasmin didn't know why that irked her, so she was glad that he was already on his way out. "Thanks for returning my cat."

————

Nico arrived late. She sat in Yasmin's living room freaking out about her friend living in the same place as *this* person. Nico kept saying it over and over.

"It's Kota!" Nico exclaimed. This was the only time Yasmin realized she didn't know *his* name. He had just been a nameless annoying blob of a person.

She had been stewing in annoyance. She thought she recognized a hint of guilt in there, though. She *should* check if he really needed shots, because what if he was just faking having anti-rabies shots already? And if he dies? *And her cat?* It was the responsible thing to do.

But why does it have to be him? It could have been *anyone* in this whole building. It could have been one of the people he lived with! Apparently there's a full group of singing and dancing men in there.

Cosmo, who brought him up to her unit, was now sleeping on the couch like he did nothing wrong.

"Have you seen the rest of them?" Nico asked, still not over it.

Yasmin shrugged, "I don't know. Probably. There are only two elevators."

She squealed at that. "How could you keep this from me? You know how much I love them. And now you're living with them!"

"I am not living with them. I am living in the same building as them." *And I reported one of them for being noisy.*

She didn't tell her friend that. She would never hear the end of it, she's sure.

"I'll visit you weekly," Nico added. "I'll bring you lunch."

Yasmin sighed, unable to fully listen to her. She was very much thinking about whether or not he did get his shots, if there was a clinic near them, and if it was available at night.

But he was a grown man, as her friend observed (she is now talking about someone's abs in this one music video?), and he should be able to take care of himself. He's a celebrity too, which meant he probably had assistants to go with him and tons of money to afford his medical bills, unlike her, a staff nurse who just started three months ago at the nearby hospital.

He's gonna make it out alive. Right?

three

. . .

THE COLD BOARDROOM was not their usual place for meetings. Boardroom meetings meant logistics, finances, and serious business stuff.

Everything else—the actual creative work—was done in recording studios, rehearsal spaces, and chats.

But it turned out that the topic for today's meeting had nothing to do with their work after all. It was about their living space.

LuvByte has been occupying the two-bedroom apartment at Roman's Court. The two rooms had two double decks: one housed four boys while the slightly smaller one had three. This wasn't the best living situation, but they understood as beginners that money wasn't there *just* yet. It was something they had to work hard for.

By year 3, things were slightly better. The topic of moving to a new place—may be a house instead of an apartment—was brought up but was put off because they were about to tour. It didn't seem too long ago, but now that Kota thought about it, it had been around this time since they started asking this question.

"I think it'd be good," Oli said, easily accepting the proposed change.

"I mean if you're all okay with it," Chili spoke, surprising Kota. As the youngest member, Chili was used to watching the older members volley for opinions before giving his own.

They started talking about it with excited voices and remarks, but Kota felt frozen in place. A nudge by his ribcage made him look at Sam, their eldest member, and the de facto leader.

"That's less for you to clean," he said with a chuckle.

While that is true and would be preferable, Kota felt a pang of sadness for what this move would entail: change. And with their contract renewal coming up in a few months, he couldn't help but feel nervous. So far, no one has expressed not renewing, and it seemed like everyone still wanted to be part of the group, but still.

He knew he could always change his mind and so as the boys. It was only fair for them to hear out other opportunities despite being in a group.

They were individual people who initially wanted to be individual artists at the end of the day. They didn't want to be part of a group, but that was the hand that was dealt, and they all took it.

Kota felt his lips move, and a peal of nervous laughter followed suit.

"We can vote, right?" Somebody finally said.

A vote. Yes. They can vote.

Miles, who had the knack for brightening the group's mood, raised his hand, "People who want to move to a new, bigger place with the possibility of having your own room, raise your hand."

Hands shot up too fast. But they were right, *it was time.* They worked their way up and should be reaping their rewards. It meant some kind of freedom, space which he so sorely missed. But how would the new living arrangement affect their relationships? Especially now that they've become so close and in sync?

Miles chuckled. "Easy."

"Are you all in a hurry to move out?" Kota asked.

Sam cleared his throat, "We have a month left in our lease. We've put this off for too long. It's either we renew or we send our 30-day notice and look for new apartments."

"I thought we were looking for a house?" He asked.

"A house would be good, but we might find one farther from the company. We need you to be close and not sit through EDSA for hours." Norah answered.

Kota nodded. That was the problem with being in Manila. There were fewer houses and more condos built. And if that was the case then that meant apartments, or condo units — *plural*. How many apartments are they talking about here? One for each? Will they be divided into two groups? Or in trios and pairs, like how they do for hotel rooms when they travel?

"I'm hungry," Sam said.

"Let's order pizza."

"Let's get chicken wings too."

Soon enough everyone was just throwing out food names until someone would pick up their phone to order it. Kota felt himself relax, leaning back in his seat. He didn't want decisions to be made rashly, so he appreciated having the diversion. A time in between was all he needed to resign to the fact that this was happening, and it was not necessarily for the worse.

Sam grabbed his phone first, the designated order taker.

"What do you want, K?"

"Whatever the group wants."

Sam's thumb paused as his eyes remained on the screen. Then, he peered at him. "Don't worry about it."

"What?"

He shook his head with a chuckle, thumb back to scrolling through a menu. "You can soundproof your room."

My room? Kota was tickled with that idea. Having a room, for himself. He didn't have to share it with anyone else. He loved these boys but he needed to sleep without Oli snoring.

"Can't let you get reported to the HAB again," Sam teased.

Kota rolled his eyes, afraid that he would never live this down.

No more walking on eggshells. No more weird cat visiting their balcony. No more noise bans.

Maybe it wasn't such a bad idea after all.

———

He would live, right?

Despite him saying that he would, Yasmin stayed up all night thinking, *what if Cosmo really has rabies?* And so she sat there and watched her cat sleep, imagining if it would start showing signs of infection.

She knew Cosmo probably didn't because he was clean and mostly indoors, but of course, there were days like yesterday when he slipped out of the apartment.

In the morning, she took Cosmo straight to the vet for his shots and asked the vet if it was possible, and the vet shrugged, "Probably not, but better safe than sorry" and left it at that.

It didn't help her worrying, and by the time she returned home with the cat carrier, she was convinced that she would drop by his unit to ask if he was feeling anything.

She may hate him, but she didn't want him to die (more importantly, have her cat die), not with him being so important (at least to Nico and a dozen other girls who are probably in love with him or something. Yuck, by the way.)

So she was relieved to see him walking into the lobby with

someone else. Probably one of *them*. The other guy was slightly familiar to her. He was taller, bulkier in his build, and impossible to ignore. She'd seen him around, mostly wearing a cap and a plain white shirt. He's usually quiet and walks around with his earbuds, minding his own business.

Next to his friend, Kota looked like the younger brother. The other one greeted Yasmin with a quick and polite nod as if it was a thing he does a lot with other residents.

Kota, on the other hand, sighed at the sight of her.

Sighed. Yasmin pressed her lips together, determined to keep herself from saying anything.

"Hello," the other guy started, and she noticed how Kota's head shot up to glare at him.

"Hi." She just said it because *he* was nicer to her.

Kota scowled at her as if her interaction with his friend was forbidden.

"You're alive," she managed to say, willing herself to be petty.

"You seem disappointed," Kota answered almost too quickly as if he was waiting for her to say something too.

An awkward silence passed between them before his friend spoke.

"Oh, you're the cat's owner." He pointed to the cat carrier. He peeked inside it, and Yasmin willingly raised it to show her cat to him.

"This is Cosmo," she said. Yasmin was not the friendliest person, but she does turn into one when people show interest in her pets. They were her pride and joy, and she could appreciate people who think the same.

"Hello Cosmo," he wiggled his hand on the carrier. "I'm Sam."

He did a cute little bow. She noticed that his eyes crinkled as he smiled.

Right, Sam. She did hear Nico talk about him and his...

Yasmin's eyes traveled from his chest to his stomach

before looking away, cursing Nico silently. She did not need to learn *this* much about people she hadn't met yet.

When she looked away, she caught Kota looking at her with another scowl, judgment evident in his eyes.

Yasmin cleared her throat, and Sam looked from her to his friend.

"My vet says you should be ok as long your vaccine is still valid." She said.

"See, you're not dying," Sam nudged him with his elbow.

"Sam!" Kota barked.

"What?" He laughed and turned to Yasmin. "He was worrying about it. He cleaned the bathroom all night from stress."

Yasmin didn't know if she was laughing because Sam had to disclose that or because Kota's face was turning bright red.

Nico wasn't kidding. Sam was charming as hell, and if *he* was the one who woke her up that day? She wouldn't mind. He would probably apologize to her right away.

The elevator door opened, and Sam nodded to tell her to take it. She smiled at him for that, this well-mannered, quiet, charming gentleman -- so unlike his friend.

"*Alright,*" Kota rolled his eyes so far back that all she could see was the white in his eyes. "Are you gonna get on the elevator or not?"

Yasmin stepped in and turned around to press the button only to find Sam pushing Kota inside the elevator.

"What, no—" He caught himself inside the elevator.

Sam peeked over to her as the doors started to close, giving her a smile "Forgot to buy something at the convenience store. See ya."

"Wait," she said, fumbling through the buttons. But she clicked the wrong one, making it close even more.

"No!" Kota stepped next to her, his fingers pressing over hers in panic. It was too late, they were already ascending.

"It's not gonna open even if you keep doing that," she

said, aware that she barely had enough space. She looked around and inched her way out of that shared corner.

Kota stopped pressing the buttons but hung his head forward. She watched him take a deep breath before turning to her. It was as if he was in slow motion. His nostrils flared. She would have laughed at how upset and frustrated he looked if they were friends and not...whatever they were now.

He looked back at her and looked...embarrassed? He cleared his throat and walked back to his usual place.

Since they hit all the buttons earlier, they had to watch the elevator door open and close on every wrong floor.

"You could press the button to —" Yasmin started.

Kota turned to her, a stride away from towering over her. She shrank in her corner as he looked at her. His face had so many questions, but no words came out.

She looked away and felt one of her hands turn into a fist.

"What's your problem?" he finally asked, eyes still boring unto her.

"What's *your* problem?" she replied because the lack of space was not helping her with her comebacks. She pushed him away with her free hand. Cosmo made a loud *meow* that made him step back.

"You've made my life very inconvenient."

"*You* made *my* life inconvenient," Yasmin stressed.

"What did I do?"

"You won't shut up," she answered, stepping forward. "You're so loud. Everything about you screams. Your hair's orange. I understand you sing for a living, fine. It's a job. I'm not gonna suck up to you just because you're a celebrity or something."

"My hair is not orange." He looked at her incredulously. That was all he could say out of all the things she said. His hair is not orange, not right now, but it seemed like it was that time they met. It had that tinge, but salons would probably call it autumn foliage or maple orange. His hair is a shade of brown now, still dyed, but it didn't stick out as much as she first saw him.

The elevator door opened to his floor, but his hands pressed the close door button.

This idiot. He did it on his floor. "That was your floor."

His jaw clenched. It was the very thing that made her want to claw his face. Lucky for him she didn't have the nails to do the damage.

"What are you thinking about?" he asked, giving her some space to breathe.

Biting your face.

She pushed him with her fisted hand. "That's all you're gonna say? Your hair's not orange?"

He paused. "What do *you* want me to say?"

"I don't know, *I'm sorry*?"

He paused and regarded her with a look that almost seemed amused. Irritated but amused -- it was so confusing that she didn't know how to react.

"For what?" He dared ask, cocking his eyebrow like this was all a joke. "Existing?"

She wanted to yell *yes!* Jesus Christ, he was so annoying. Everything about his face was just so…

Kota smiled at her, and it was so disarming because it seemed like a genuine smile. His face was so different when he smiles, it made him seem approachable and friendly, not like the person she met that first time.

He shook his head softly. "Look, I woke you up with my voice. Your cat scratched me. Quits na tayo."

Yasmin jerked her head back. "That's not even…"

That was *not* the same thing. Cosmo is her cat, but she didn't tell him to go and scratch him? He probably deserved it for aggravating her cat.

He gazed back at the elevator door. Yasmin's attention diverted to it too. Was the elevator no longer moving?

She stepped forward and pressed the Open Door button after realizing that the screen above no longer showed which floor they were on.

"What did you press earlier?" She demanded as panic rose in her throat.

"This button," he pointed at the Close Door button.

Yasmin kept pressing the open button. "Why is it not opening?"

"Be serious."

"Do you think I'm kidding right now?" she yelled, pressing the button again.

He pulled his phone from his jeans pocket and sighed.

"Please tell me you have some sort of signal."

four

. . .

IT TOOK a couple of minutes before someone from the elevator intercom spoke, and they both ran to the speaker. Thank God, security had their eyes on the elevator cameras, and people started to wonder why the other elevator was not working.

They chose to be quiet as they managed their own mounting panic. Or at least, that was what Yasmin was doing. Cosmo kept meowing loudly, and it echoed inside the box.

She soothed the cat, took it out of its carrier, and watched it saunter at Kota's legs. He looked at the cat, then back at her.

"Cosmo, come here."

She knew the cat would do what it wanted, so it remained to circle Kota's leg, his little head rubbing his shin.

Traitor. You hated that man.

Kota didn't move, stuck on his side as he held on to the railing.

Yasmin stood and took the cat, carrying it in her arms. "Sorry."

He waved a hand, avoiding eye contact with her. She rolled her eyes at that but noticed his hand trembling on the railing.

"Are you okay?"

He raised his hand, waving her off again like he would like to be left alone, "I'll be okay once the door opens."

"You're not claustrophobic, are you?"

"Nope," he answered, his other hand gripping the railing too. "How long did they say it's gonna take before the door opens?"

"5 or 10 minutes," she shrugged.

He let out a shuddering breath.

"If you're having a panic attack —"

"Shh," he said, his eyes closed. "Please just be quiet."

Yasmin scoffed at the implication that *she* was the noisy one in this very tiny box. Her cat started purring so she stayed on her side, faced the wall, and pretended that she didn't mind being stuck there for what felt like an hour.

At last, the door slightly opened, and the maintenance man said hello to them. They were in the middle of the floor and had to climb through a bit to get out of there.

She heard Kota curse under his mouth.

Seriously, what is wrong with him? The maintenance dropped a block to make it easier for them to climb up, and Kota positioned himself first.

"Really?" She said aloud, "*Ladies first* doesn't ring any bell?"

He paused, bowed his head, then stepped back to motion her towards it.

"It doesn't work if I had to tell you."

"I am begging you to please just go." He had a very stiff mouth now like he was doing his best not to break or…

She paused and passed her cat to the maintenance man without taking her eyes off him. With narrowed eyes, she asked, "Are you taking a shit?"

His eyes shot daggers. She raised her hands and mouthed *fine* before pulling herself up.

She was on her floor, thank God, and didn't know if she

had to wait for him. When he stepped out, he thanked the maintenance man, bowed his head almost, then started running.

He stopped midway when he realized this wasn't his floor. Their eyes met, and somehow, with his eyes wide and mouth dry, she finally understood.

She ran to her door, basically dropping her cat on the floor. Her fingers trembled to get the keys, and when it finally unlocked, she pushed her door open and yelled, "Here."

He rushed to her side, ran inside, and straight to her toilet.

She would need to give him a pair of pants, a towel, or something.

———

Kota's Most Embarrassing Moments

- Broke a trophy while still accepting the award in front of 20,000 people.
- Slipped in the hallway with other trainees laughing at him.
- Had to kiss Yuan with a blindfold as punishment at a variety show, almost kissed him on the lips, ON TV. It has 6 million views on YouTube, the last time Chili joked about it.
- …The orange hair. Maybe. He was called Kiat Kiat for a while. He didn't mind it so much until today.
- Holding his pee for minutes only to lose it before he could lift the toilet lid. On his nemesis' toilet.

———

"Um," Yasmin listened to the sound of water running from her bathroom. She stood outside, noting that there was some scrubbing happening in there. She knocked on the door cautiously.

He opened the door, face more relaxed. She didn't mean to, but she gazed down at his pants and then back at him.

"What's…" She didn't know what to ask him. How to phrase it. *How?*

"I cleaned your bathroom."

"I heard it." She peered inside, her head bumping with his chest for a bit. He leaned back, and that reaction made her cringe. She looked away and cleared her throat. "I smelled it, actually."

The smell of Zonrox was overpowering.

Kota stepped to the side, no longer holding her bathroom hostage.

"Sorry, I clean when I get stressed," he explained. "I made a bit of a mess."

She smirked, closing the light and the door of the bathroom. "Spare me the details."

"Gladly."

"Can you come up here when stressed?" She bit her tongue as soon as she said, wincing at herself. He looked at her, confused. "Sorry. Joking. You just cleaned it so well. I won't mind paying someone for that."

"Oh." He straightened his back.

It was a weird compliment — if it even sounded like one — but she sure wasn't expecting him to clean her bathroom.

He was weirder for that, she decided. And it warranted the compliment she gave.

"Sorry for uh," Kota looked down, and she wanted to commend him for being able to show his face after that. She knew some people would be so embarrassed that they'd misplace their frustration or anger on somebody else. He was surprisingly calm though, almost regretful? "Sorry for snapping at you in the elevator."

Oh. She didn't expect that. She thought he was apologizing for messing up her bathroom, even though he already made up for that.

"And for using your stuff," he pointed to the bathroom door, "I can replace the —"

"Dude," she cut him off.

His eyes lifted to meet hers, surprised that she was addressing him casually.

Yasmin walked past him, and he followed her to face her still. She looked at him and made the decision. She offered a handshake.

He looked at her hand, then at her, then back at it, a relieved smile forming on his lips. *Ah yes, one of those smiles again.* What a rare sighting.

His hand took hers and clasped it, not too loose that it seemed insincere and not too tight that it was overbearing.

They shook hands.

"You washed your hands, right?" She had to do it. It was getting too serious.

He rolled his eyes, "Shut up."

Surprisingly, they both laughed. Not at each other, but *with* each other. He slowly let go of her hand.

Yasmin smiled at him. "*Now* we can call it quits."

five

. . .

IT IS a truth universally acknowledged that Filipinos love to sing. Most could carry a tune and treat videoke as their pastime.

Kota didn't always know he could sing, but he started finding out really young. His mom would take him to Christmas parties to sing "Christmas in Our Hearts," and that would make him super rich for a five-year-old during Christmas.

Then, the school started doing talent shows, and that was when he fell in love with performing. He liked how it made him feel: the rush of getting to the stage, the look on people's faces as he sang. A lot of things didn't make sense for Kota as a teenager, but being on stage was not one of them. It was *the* only thing that made sense. So when everyone else was thinking about applying to Universities, he was looking at auditions.

Even if he was good, being a professional singer was extremely competitive. Sure, he could have just started a YouTube channel and sang his songs there to get discovered, but Kota wanted the whole nine yards. The record deal, the touring, the albums, the awards, the merch, the TV appearances — and he got it all, eventually, with the help of 6 other boys.

He didn't always think of being in a team, but when he was put in one, he quickly shifted that mindset and did things *for* the team.

Even if that meant yelling at them in the morning for a call time.

"Kota, shut up!" Yuan yelled at him, covering his entire face with a blanket.

"I would if you get up now." He tugged at the blanket.

Yuan was always the hardest one to wake up. The rest of the boys can wake up with a shake or a tap.

"I'm reporting you to HAB."

That whole ordeal has been an ongoing joke with the group now, and it probably added as a reason why Kota was so annoyed by it all.

"Ha-ha, *three minutes,*" he said sharply. "We can leave without you. I'm not kidding."

Yuan just grumbled and kicked him out off the edge of his bed.

He stepped out of the room and found Sam carrying Kota's guitar. "Why is this out?"

"I'm not talking to you."

"You're still mad at me?"

"Mom and Dad are fighting," Oli interrupted. Being the group's parents was also an inside joke, but Kota did not appreciate it today. It's always chaos in the mornings, especially when they need to leave in 20 minutes.

"You pushed me inside an elevator." Kota frowned.

"I nudged you." Sam clarified.

"I was stuck in that elevator for fifteen minutes."

"And I'm sorry you had to experience that," Sam answered. "But I didn't stop the elevator from operating. Now, who are you serenading?"

"No one." He took the guitar from him.

"You were playing Harana."

"It's the easiest thing to play." It was also probably one of the only songs he remembered playing, as it was one of his firsts. Parokya ni Edgar was always a hit in the classrooms.

"Stop pissing off the neighbor upstairs."

"I'm not. We called it quits yesterday."

"Then you should thank me?" Sam folded his arms across his chest.

Kota, on the other hand, stuck his tongue out. "No. I told you I'd just use the stairs. You told me to get on the elevator with you so it would be faster."

"It is faster."

"No, it isn't."

"How is that my fault?"

Kota rolled his eyes instead. He was done with the argument. Yes, that wasn't Sam's fault, but he still didn't need to force him to get on that elevator. While he's relieved that the Goddess didn't seem mad at him anymore, Kota worried that she found him humorous and felt sorry for him instead.

He turned his back and winced at that thought, still haunted by yesterday's events. He barely slept, which was also why he woke everyone up earlier than needed.

Surprisingly, Yuan dragged his ass from his bed and out the door. Kota was expecting to yell at him for ten more minutes.

"I heard that there was fighting," Yuan rubbed his eyes.

"It's a quiet one." Kota bit back.

"Ten minutes," Sam told Yuan sternly. The boy pretty much scampered to the bathroom with his order.

"You should wake everyone up instead." Kota sighed.

"No way," Sam answered. "You do it so much better."

"And just because I do it better, I'm supposed to wake up earlier than everyone else?"

He was feeling pricklier than usual. A part of him was

already regretting opening his mouth, but another part wanted to remain sulky and mad.

"Okay, time out." Sam caught up with him and pulled on his shoulder.

"Not right now." Kota forcefully moved his hand away.

But Sam is stronger. The man is calm but he could crack a coconut open with his bare hands. Kota had seen it before.

He felt Sam's arms circle around his chest and lifted him off the ground.

Oh, here we go. He was gonna fight back. He had this pent-up energy for it. He kicked Sam's shin soon as he put him back down. Kota turned and found Sam charging at him, then heard a loud *thud* as he blinked his eyes. He heard the others scuffle out of their rooms.

Kota rolled on his back, realizing they were both on the floor. Their eyes met for a second before acknowledging that they were done with his ridiculous display of misplaced anger. Sam let him go and eventually helped him up.

"Sorry," Sam said first as he tapped Kota's arm.

"Sorry," he answered as he rubbed his shoulder.

"Do you still need to punch something, or are you good?" Kota sighed.

There had been fights in the house before, of course, but they try their best to not make it physical. They bicker a lot and chase each other, but they made a pact to not resent and hurt each other.

"Payment jar is there." Oli reminded them. They had payment jars as part of the system in case of fights, for being late, or for breaking a rule. Then they use the money to buy themselves food.

"I am *not* missing this when we move out," Chili murmured.

Sam raised his hands and Kota sighed. They also vowed all fights should end with a hug because of camaraderie, teamwork, and all that.

They hugged for a bit.

Sam patted his back, "You know I appreciate everything you do for us."

He nodded.

"I'll take care of the boys. Go for a walk or something. I will buy us some time. See you downstairs."

———

He didn't go for a walk. Kota felt like he didn't need to be seen, at least not yet. So he sat in silence in the emergency exit stairway. Emergency Exits are great escape routes. As a trainee in the company, Kota had frequented the stairs to get a bit of quiet.

Not a lot of people use the stairs, and if they do, they usually just pass through.

Kota felt slightly ashamed of what had happened with Sam earlier. They don't condone fights but also know it could happen. Still, he didn't want it to be with *him*.

He let out a sigh, a loud one at that, as he stretched his arms up. He hoped no bruises showed up later. He didn't want Steph, their makeup artist, to say something.

He heard some footsteps from the floor above so he made himself tiny, scooting to the side of the steps. He didn't want to look like he was waiting for that person to come down, but he couldn't help but look up.

She did a little swivel when their eyes met. Her foot hesitated and then turned.

Kota looked down, aware that her hesitation was because of him.

There was an awkward silence before she greeted him with a polite "Hey."

He looked up again and noticed that she was wearing a scrub suit. It's the first time that he took note of that. Previously, he only saw her in casual clothes (and even sleepwear, if he was going to count that first time they met). The uniform affected him and made him consider her differently.

He respected healthcare workers and knew how hard it was to be in the field. He had a couple of friends who went on to study Nursing for college and heard about their struggles.

"I didn't wanna use the elevator. In case, you know…" she explained.

He nodded in agreement. *He* wouldn't want to either. When he left her unit yesterday, he also used the stairs.

She smirked and then awkwardly waved at him to say goodbye.

And then that was that. She was gone in a matter of seconds, and he had the space to himself again.

He let out a breath—one he didn't know he held as she left—and stood from his seat. *That wasn't as bad,* he thought. It was awkward, but it was better than how it used to be. He felt tense and self-conscious with her, but now he just felt…well, he was still self-conscious, but she didn't hate him anymore. That was less burden for him to carry.

Kota returned to their unit in time for everyone else to leave.

———

They met in the stairwell a couple more times, but there were no more barking or snide comments. She meant it when she called it quits with him then. Perhaps it was how he carried himself after the event that made her change her mind.

He apologized to her for how he acted in the elevator, which meant he knew when he made a mistake and would take accountability for it.

He didn't apologize for the noise that day— she didn't agree with him, but she could respect him enough to know that he was capable of apologizing genuinely.

It was a misunderstanding, Yasmin had to remind herself.

And people *will* misunderstand. She knew this all too well. She lived long enough to know that people can continue to do that, even if you tried to explain. What mattered to her more was people who *can* recognize a mistake and admit it.

There were days when she returned from the hospital bone-tired and restless, and somehow hearing his voice through the stairwell put her at ease. Some days she felt like it was pulling her legs up so she could finally come home—to her bed and her cat.

This week, he had been away for three days, and Yasmin wondered if he was not around or just stopped hanging around the Emergency Exit. He could have been over his elevator panic by now.

It wasn't until later that Nico told her that LuvByte was in Bangkok to perform at a music festival. She didn't ask for this information, but she felt great relief in knowing that he was just away for work. He did not abandon this weird new habit of meeting each other in the stairwell.

As she set off for work the next day, she noticed him in his spot—early in the morning, with a takeaway cup of coffee in his hand.

He looked up at her the moment he heard the door from her floor close as if he was waiting for her to show up.

Yasmin grabbed the railing and noted how he smiled at her. It was like he was waiting for her, and she was someone he wanted to see.

She paused on the landing where he sat and spoke. "You're alive."

"You don't sound disappointed."

Yasmin didn't know how to respond to that, so she simply gave him a nod.

He took something from his pocket and said, "Catch!"

Her reflexes were sharp enough to catch it, but they both laughed at the suddenness of it all.

Yasmin opened her hand and saw a piece of sweet chili

tamarind. *Token Thai pasalubong.* Yet she had to pretend that she didn't know about his trip. It would be too creepy if she revealed that.

"Thanks?" she looked at the candy and then at him. "You look tired."

He raised his cup of coffee. "Hence."

She felt the urge to sit next to him like they were two old friends meeting to catch up.

"Busy day?" she asked.

Kota rubbed his eyes, "No, just…thought I'd come here. For a bit."

Yasmin smiled and gave in to the desire to sit next to him. She busied herself with opening the tamarind candy but her fingers shook.

His hands enveloped hers for a moment, took that candy from her hands to open it. He tore the wrapper with his teeth and handed it back to her.

She took it and left the wrapper in his hand, which he tucked in his pocket after. She popped it in her mouth and felt his eyes on her the entire time.

Yasmin winced, "Oh, there's a kick to it."

"I hate it," he said.

"Then why would you give it to me?" she pushed him, and he let out a laugh.

"You might like it."

"I do like it."

"See?"

Yasmin shook her head but was aware that she still had a smile on. "I have to go to work."

She stood and readied herself to go.

"You know what's funny?" he started again.

She arched a brow in response.

"I don't even know your name," He said. And it was true; it's not like she introduced herself to him at the HAB office.

She was referred to as Ms. Guerra, but maybe he didn't catch that.

Yasmin hesitated in giving her name away as if that would make *things* progress. She didn't know if she wanted that.

"I'm Kota," he said. It was so cute how he said it too like he didn't think that she would know him by now, that her friend wasn't just yapping about him, that she couldn't just type his name on a search bar and have thousands of results.

"Yasmin," she finally said. She watched his face brighten, and it felt good to receive his smile.

It was just a name but she felt like she'd permitted him to get to know her beyond their first impressions.

"See you tomorrow, Yasmin."

six

. . .

HE SHOULD PROBABLY STOP CALLING her Goddess now that she'd given her real name to him, but somehow, having her real name seemed more precious to him.

Kota didn't drop her name when Oli asked about the neighbor upstairs earlier, he simple answered his question and left out the fact that her given name is *Yasmin*.

They could find that out on their own, as far as he's concerned. He earned that as well as that laugh she let out this morning.

She had been in his mind during the spare moments they had, in between the rehearsals and the shuffling from the airport to hotels to the venue. He thought about the color she'd be wearing that day like he was playing a game of *"What color would Yasmin wear next?"*

She looked beautiful in yellow. Kota loved seeing her hair down but also liked the shape of her neck whenever she wore her hair up. *There he goes again.* He had to stop visualizing her. He used to avoid her, never even wanted to breathe near her, but now? Kota couldn't help but seek her out, even if that meant sitting in the stairway longer than he had to. *Just in case he runs into her again.*

And Yasmin has been pretty consistent. He didn't know if it was because she genuinely hated the elevator, or if she's been looking forward to running into him as much as he had.

Kota wanted it to be the latter so badly but didn't want to smother her with his curiosities. And so sometimes, he would just say a thing or two, and leave it at that. He knew *when* to stop, gauge if she was comfortable with it or not.

They've been developing…*something*, he couldn't quite tell yet. For him, it was this mounting desire to please her, to get her approval, like he was still so bent on the fact that she was the only one who complained about him.

Kota wanted to show her that he was not the person she thought he was, but even with that agenda, he also started to find her amusing. He wanted to know more about her.

Her eyes softened when she looked at him, and Kota noticed how her voice seemed sweeter and kinder. It could be just him, but he couldn't help but think that she was also interested in him.

If she didn't report him to HAB, would he have met her at all? He didn't pay that much attention to people—especially when he was in public. He started to feel guilty about his non-work hours, always hurried to get from place to place with the mission of not getting noticed, covering his face as much as possible.

He would still be nice though. He would help someone cross the street or answer someone if they needed directions —but it would be a fleeting moment. He'd run away soon after to get to his destination.

This might be the only time in so long that he started to linger, staying put so he could learn and be learned.

On this day, Yasmin appeared on the stairway with her hair tucked in a low ponytail. He watched the hair swish from side to side and smiled at her peach-colored scrubs.

"Hi," she greeted first.

"Hello."

Yasmin clutched the strap of her bag.

"Did you hear me down there?" he asked. He had been listening to the song he would be recording soon, taking note of the spots where he could sing his adlibs. His recording goes faster when he's better prepared.

"Just a little bit." She raised her hand to gesture.

"How'd I sound?"

"Huh?"

He sang the quick adlib that he was working on. He wanted to know if he should keep the runs or cut it short.

"I—I'm not qualified for that." She fiddled with her hands.

"You have ears, right?" he teased. But genuinely, he wanted to know what she thought.

Instead, she gave him a smirk, and it made him want to pinch her for being so...*her*. They have stopped attacking each other, but there is a playfulness between them that he enjoyed.

"No, I got rid of them yesterday." She smiled sarcastically.

Uy, you like her. That was it, wasn't it? He had said so many things but it all comes down to that. He liked her. He liked her so much.

"You sound fine," she said instead, another nugget of hope that she liked him back.

"You like the first one or the second?"

She tilted her head to think for a second. "The first one."

"I should work harder then," Kota said.

She raised a brow.

"I wanted to sound great." He gave her a smile before going back to his notes. Kota decided that that was enough for today, even when he wanted to pull on her hand and make her sit next to him.

She could make that decision any time, and he would be there, no matter what.

———

Nico visited her that weekend, disappointed that none of the LuvByte boys used the elevators as she made her way up. Yasmin laughed at this, knowing too well that one of them had at least stopped doing that.

But she wouldn't say that.

It would be weird to take her friend to the Emergency Exit, it would feel like breaking the trust she had established with Kota. That stairwell was somehow their safe space, one where they could both hide from the outside.

"What's going on with you?" her friend suddenly asked while they were eating their noodles.

"What?" she cut the noodles with her teeth and let them plop down her bowl.

"You seem to be in a better mood these days."

Oh. Yasmin straightened her back. There wasn't any particular reason why she seemed to be in a better mood. Work was fine and she no longer feared coming across the annoying neighbor downstairs. She looked forward to seeing him instead. She recently spent her mornings wishing he would be there, so she could catch him before she left for work. He wasn't her annoying neighbor anymore, he was Kota.

She felt a smile come up on her lips with just the thought.

"I'm not on the night shift," she reasoned, which was also true. She hated being on the night shift, and having her life back on normal hours made her happy.

Her friend believed that, and she was thankful that Nico didn't pry about her sudden and developing fondness for her friend's third favorite LuvByte member (there was a ranking, and yes, Sam is first. Yasmin understood this completely and have no comments).

Yasmin joined Nico in the elevator as she made her way out of the building and watched her get to her cab before coming back up. She used the stairs, and almost sprinted up, hoping that he was there, sitting on the stairs, probably with his earphones and notes.

Yasmin liked to prove herself right, and when she made her way to the landing, their eyes seemed to both lift, meeting for the first time today.

He smiled at her and she returned it immediately. She was aware of how these little run-ins in the stairway were becoming the highlight of her day. She didn't feel too bad about letting herself have that. There are so few pleasures and this became hers.

She placed her hand on her jacket's pocket as she climbed, then threw him a mini orange. He didn't catch it (she should have given him a heads-up) so he picked it up instead.

"The hospital had them." She explained.

Kota examined the orange in his hand, "They called me Kiat Kiat that time my hair was orange."

She sat next to him and pulled another orange from her pocket.

"How many are in there?"

She laughed and pulled three more, offering it to him.

He started to peel the skin, stopped to smell the scent, and praised it. He popped the whole thing in his mouth.

"What?" he asked as he chewed.

"*That's* how you eat it?"

"It's tiny." He swallowed the fruit before taking another one, tearing the skin efficiently. Kota offered it to her.

"No, I ate like three of those earlier."

"Then why do you have more?" He looked at her jacket's pocket like he was expecting more oranges to come out of it.

"They made me take them home." It wasn't a lie. But she also thought she could give it to him if she ever ran into him. Which she did. Again, she was right. And she loved being right about things.

He tore the orange in half and offered it to her again, raising it closer to her mouth.

She took it, leaning over to bite into it, her lips briefly touching the tip of his finger. He ate the rest of it and kissed his fingers.

"Should I be welcoming you with snacks when you come up here then?"

"Don't be silly."

"A Gatorade for your workout."

She paused, "Actually, that would be nice."

Kota laughed. "Tomorrow. Okay."

She shifted to stand, turning slightly to him. "See you."

"Mmm." he nodded, raising a hand to say goodbye to her.

seven

. . .

BUT HE WASN'T THERE the next day. It should have worried Yasmin when she felt disappointed, but she reminded herself that he didn't promise to be there. She knew that he had a different schedule than her. He had a different lifestyle even.

She found herself looking up his name on the internet that day, and it felt wrong to her that she could access this much information about a person. So she stopped that and decided to take Cosmo out for a walk. Yasmin somehow wished that she could go back to how it was—*not* when she hated him and everything he did seemed to annoy her. She rather preferred the time she didn't know him. It was better then.

It was so weird to see him as a celebrity and also know him as the person he was. They just seemed to be two separate concepts that she couldn't fit together yet.

When she returned to Roman's Court, she took the elevator for the first time in a couple of weeks and felt good about that. She had no business looking him up on the internet, and even looking forward to hearing his voice.

She used to *not* want to hear his voice.

How did she get here?

In a few hours, she woke up from a prolonged nap and found Cosmo staring at her. He let out a loud purr before jumping off the sofa. That was when Yasmin realized that she slept through the rest of her late afternoon and missed Cosmo's usual dinner time.

"Thanks for waking me up," she told the cat, turning the lights on.

She fed the cat, refilled his water bowl, and cleaned the litter. She changed into her pajamas and decided to have a Cup Noodle and watch TV.

An hour passed before there was a knock on her door. Yasmin and Cosmo turned to each other, but the cat simply blinked and walked away to sleep.

Yasmin checked the time: *11 pm*. Who in their right mind still knocks on people's doors at 11? Maybe if she just lowered the volume of her TV and ignore it, they would go away.

Another quick knock.

She quietly walked to the door, aiming to peek through the eyehole. She caught the back of his head, and quickly opened her door.

He jumped at the sound of that and turned to her with a bit of surprise in his face.

"How'd you know I was awake?" she asked.

"Your light's on." He pointed inside, and she realized that he could probably see that through their balcony.

"Oh." Yasmin noticed that he was carrying a little pail with cleaning tools.

He seemed to follow her line of sight and explained, "You told me to come up here when I'm stressed."

Oh. He took that seriously. But more importantly, "Why are you stressed?"

Kota looked stressed just from that question. His brows furrowed and his shoulders dropped. "I don't wanna talk about it when I'm stressed."

"So…you just want to clean?"

He snapped his fingers, "Exactly. I already cleaned ours, so…"

"Were there other bathrooms in the running?" She asked.

The side of Kota's lips lifted, and she watched as he gave her an amused smile, as if what she asked was so funny for him. "No. I'll probably do the laundry if this option is not available."

Yasmin leaned at the door frame for a good second, assessing if this was a good idea. But she also…wanted to see him. She did not open her door so quickly just to make him do laundry at 11 PM.

"You're a weird man, do you know that?"

He took that as a *yes* on cleaning and pushed himself inside her house.

"I can talk about it after," he said, back turned to her. "Maybe. If you wanna hear it. I don't know."

"Kota," she called him. His brows raised in response. "Nothing. We can talk about it later."

She didn't plan to stay up all night, but she waited for him on the couch, pretending that she cared enough about what was on TV. The late-night news is almost ending, and that's always her cue to clean up and go back to her room to sleep.

At last, after a few minutes, he came out, gloves in hand with his trusty pail of cleaning materials. Yasmin let Kota set those aside before talking to him.

"Did that help?" she asked and watched him nod.

He took a step closer to the couch. "What are you watching?"

It was time for Home TV Shopping. It featured the Tornado Mop which genuinely piqued his interest.

Yasmin laughed at his expression, mouth formed into an O when the mop squeezed out the water.

She didn't mind that he softly plopped himself on the couch's armrest.

"Aren't cats supposed to be nocturnal?" He asked a while later.

He pointed to Cosmo in his cage, all curled up.

"I let him out when I go to sleep," Yasmin explained. "Usually he just chases lizards or bugs, if he ever found one inside."

"Good pesticide control."

"Yeah," she agreed. "Am I turning you into a cat person?"

He smirked, eyes still fixed on Cosmo. "Maybe."

"You're like a dog though," she said. "That sounds like an insult. I promise you it's not."

"Complimenting *is* a skill." Kota laughed.

"I *can* compliment people," she protested. "Your friend Sam is very charming."

He made a face.

"Do you do this a lot?"

"Clean our neighbors' bathrooms?" Kota laughed.

"No, knock on women's doors at night?"

"Oh." He straightened his back. "No."

Yasmin rested her head on her arm, not sure what to say next. Their gazes met as they sat through a peaceful quiet.

She didn't know exactly how it came to be — perhaps it began with their fingers clutching each other, their limbs entangling, and then—*then.*

Their lips met, and it was so soft and tentative at first. The hesitation came from her waiting for him to tell her he wanted it.

She wanted it.

A silent moment passed, their noses touching for a second, breathing in each other. She opened her eyes and found him looking intently at her and finding the answer then and there.

Kota wanted her.

It was all she needed to move, shifting from her seat to climb up to his lap and straddle him.

A smile broke out on Kota's face and it was new to her:

mischievous, playful, cocky, almost. She touched his cheek, her thumb running along his whisker dimple, aware that she had been cataloging his smiles since she started receiving them.

It was his smile that made her change her mind—or heart—and this damned imperfection on his left cheek that made him...

"So cute," she said out loud.

Kota watched her with an amused grin. His hand ran through her hair and tucked the loose hair behind her ear.

He kissed her thumb when she lowered it from his cheek, and she took it as her cue to kiss him again because *why did they stop?* Kota softly ran his hands on her back. His fingertips tugged the hem of her shirt, and it felt like an eternity before he finally slipped his hands under.

She let out a giggle with this, in between their kisses, and he kept rewarding her with these new smiles that she needed to identify: *Kota's smile when he's teased, Kota's smile when I bite his lip, Kota's smile when he realized I wasn't wearing a bra.*

"Bedroom," she said. It's not a complete sentence, but they both understood. They got up from the couch. There was a moment of shyness as she led the way to her bedroom, a place no man had been in since she moved here.

Her hand stretched out to him, and he took it with his slender fingers. He held on to her until they reached their destination.

The light from the window was enough for them to move through the space. She pulled him over, falling and landing on the mattress with a soft laugh.

Through the soft light, their eyes met. Their faces were so close that they started to whisper assurances. He asked her if she was alright, and she nodded, feeling the warmth spread from her core through her whole body.

Kota's hands reached under her shirt again, and she did him the favor of lifting herself off the bed so he could take it off her. He kissed her again, his hands on her face before they traveled to her neck and breasts. He pulled her up, arms wrapped in her waist as he took one breast with his mouth.

She was startled at the sensation, slightly embarrassed at her reaction. Kota paused to look up and asked her if she was okay, and honestly, *he was so hot for that*. Yasmin tugged at his shirt because fair is fair, and she needed him to be naked like yesterday.

He was quick to follow, but when she started to yank his pants off, he held her hand and whispered, "No, not so fast, Goddess. We'll be here for a while."

She blushed and felt the warmth in her cheeks but even more so in her core. Her hand reached to her sex, and he paused to watch her run her fingers over the cloth.

"Touch me," she pulled his hand and placed it where she was touching. His breath moved through her neck and his hand was warm under her, slowly and deliciously moving through her clothing. She was damp between her legs, and he was biding his time.

He called her beautiful — she heard it once or twice — between the kisses, the sucking, and the biting that made her feel like he was branding the word to her skin.

He pushed her back on the bed, and she closed her eyes and bit her lips, savoring every sensation. She willed herself to remember all this: *every touch, every kiss, every caress.*

"Open your eyes," he said. Yasmin did so as he pulled her pajama bottoms down. By instinct, her hips raised to give him all the access he needed to pleasure her and to please him. "Look at me."

She folded her legs and let them rest on his shoulders, arms propped up to do what he asked. Kota kissed the inside of her thighs, then her mound, his breath hot against her panties.

"Oh, my god." She heard herself say. She probably said

that too many times today. She needs to find a new — "Puta ka. Please. Pleasepleaseplease."

"What?" Kota laughed, in between her legs, the savage man that he is.

"Please," she said, quieter but much more desperate than she wanted to sound, but she was on the edge. She didn't want it to end, but she also wanted him to just do it already. He pulled her panties off and ran his tongue inside her fold. She threw her head back and groaned.

"You — *you*," Yasmin couldn't find the rest of the words. She gave up soon as she felt his fingers spread her out, his tongue on its quest to pleasure her clit.

He savored her there, head between her legs. Her hips buckled, and she rocked to the rhythm of the waves that came with every flick of his tongue. His arms held onto her legs as she quivered, providing her the anchor she needed when she finally let the most powerful wave crash into her, forcing a cry of pain and joy.

Release and relief coursed through her, and his hand reached out to her mouth to muffle the sound of her cry.

It made her laugh in between her ragged breaths as Kota pulled himself up to her. His face was triumphant and proud, laughing with her at the moment.

He kissed her throat softly. "Well, then. Who's the loud one now?"

———

She made him sing. He was still doing it too, as he lay on her bed, his fingers circling the skin on her arm.

She fell asleep with her head on his chest, her right hand softly on his rib. They were talking before she fell asleep, and Kota was relieved that she didn't ask him to leave. They cleaned up together, and she lent him an extra towel and a toothbrush like they were in an official sleepover. As if he didn't have all of his stuff just downstairs.

It's not like he wanted to go back to his bed. He voluntarily went to *her* bed, rubbed her back, and listened to her talk about her day before drifting off to sleep.

Now he was watching the sun rise through her window.

The boys would be looking for him any time now, but Kota didn't want to move to reach for his phone. Yasmin's cat had also walked in a couple of times, challenging him to a staring competition before it gave up.

He felt like the cat was judging him, and it was too bad that he couldn't tell the feline that she approved of him so much last night. It probably heard them. It probably stressed the cat out.

He said sorry to her cat instead and decided to get up. The cat jumped next to him, and rubbed its head on his shin, almost making him trip.

He stopped by its cage and found a little container with his kibble.

"Should I feed you?"

The cat let out a meow and he took that as a yes. He put a scoop into its bowl and watched it eat.

"I guess you like me too now?" Kota mused and ran his hand over the cat's fur.

He laughed at how funny it was. Here he was, in his neighbor's apartment, feeding her cat. No one could have predicted this, not even him, but he had no complaints.

Kota hummed a song and returned to Yasmin's bedroom where she still slept. He was comfortable in her space, still basking in the glow of their orgasms. He couldn't believe it and yet…he could, because no woman has occupied his brain space since Yasmin. It was so jarring at first that it made him want to resent her.

But it wasn't her fault. She was beautiful and irresistible, and of course, he would fall for her. *Of course*. It was almost ridiculous of him not to.

He climbed back to bed and allowed himself to doze off in between. When he woke up, he found her awake and sitting up next to him.

Kota blinked, then yawned.

"Are you hungry?" she asked.

Yes. He was dreaming of a breakfast buffet, and he was still picking through the selection when he woke up.

"What are you craving right now?" she asked, lowering herself back down so they could be face to face.

"You," he teased, and they both cringed at that, sharing a laugh. But this is what their relationship is shaping up to be: teasing and making fun of each other *with* each other.

"Yuck." She bit his shoulder playfully. "I want pancakes. Oh no, waffles."

"You know that that's almost the same thing?"

"I don't have a waffle maker," she yawned.

"But you have the batter?"

"Yes."

He lifted himself, "How long were you up?"

"A while. I fed the cat," she explained. "He was practically licking my face earlier."

"I fed him earlier too," He rubbed his eye. "He was giving me a judgy face."

"That's just how cats are," Yasmin snorted. "But he's probably weirded out that there's a strange man in my room."

"Eggs?"

"Hmm?"

"Batter, eggs?" Kota asked.

"Yes, I think." Yasmin sat up. "Are you gonna make them?"

"Sure." He didn't want to leave the bed but she wanted to be fed so that's what he'll do. *Especially after last night.* He should make sure she's hydrated too.

She playfully gasped. "Oh my god, he cooks too?"

He laughed as he quickly got up and put his pants back on. He didn't want to bother with his shirt yet, he was just making pancakes, and he can always jump back in bed. Maybe. If she still wanted him to. He can make her pancakes so fast, and eat syrup off of her breasts.

Just the thought of it made him hard, so he hurried toward the door.

"Cleans and cooks," she mused. He felt her eyes follow him as he walked over to the other side of the room. "What else can you do?"

"Make you come." He threw her a look, and the satisfaction that he felt was almost instant.

Her eyes darted away from his gaze, cheeks turning red. Her fingers fumbled on the sheet. Kota knew then that he had to be so smitten by her, all he wanted to do was to bite her shoulder and wrap her up in his arms. His instincts traipse on ravishing and/or holding her, there was no in-between.

"I can make you come too," she said, a beat too late, but still, delivered. He dropped his hand from the doorknob.

That, she did. And that, she will.

eight

. . .

THE NEXT FOUR days were a happy blur of Kota knocking on her door at night. He would appear sans the cleaning tools he brought the first night they slept together. He was more forward with it by now, his confidence growing every night.

Like today — she opened the door and he kissed her without so much as a Hi, only greeting after he had her up on the wall.

"Sorry, I'm late," he added, before letting her slide off the wall and back to Earth with him. They didn't have a set time for these meetings, but she was the fool who stared at her door every 9 PM willing him to come.

"Long day?" she asked.

Kota nodded as he walked over to her couch, where they sometimes sit and talk before taking off each other's clothes. Cosmo seemed to warm up to Kota too; the cat has been greeting him with soft purrs while walking between his legs.

"My shift changes next week," she informed him. That meant if he knocked on her door at night, she wouldn't be there to open the door for him.

He grabbed her hand and pulled her down the couch with him. "What's your next shift like?"

"6 PM to 2 AM." Yasmin lifted her feet on the couch, and he grabbed it to put it over his lap. *So handsy, so clingy.* He's an acts-of-service-as-love-language kind of person, she recognized early on. Kota would bring her water in the middle of the night, or after they had sex, would cook her breakfast before leaving her apartment, and would always pleasure her first before pleasuring himself.

But touch was something he enjoyed, she realized. He liked it when she rubbed his shoulder, ran her hand through his hair, or even drape her leg on his lap, like *this*.

"Ah yes, the shift that made you want to kill me."

She was on that shift when she was woken up by Kota's voice that morning. She was just falling asleep when he started singing that same note. It didn't help that she was on her period then, so everything hurt, and everything annoyed her.

"I'll be quiet," he said.

She kissed him on the cheek as a thank you in advance. Who would've thought she'd go from hating him to wanting to kiss him silly in a matter of few days? Yasmin let out a giggle, which he caught and asked about.

"Did you hate me too?" Yasmin asked.

Kota shook his head. "Not hate, more like frustrated. Intimidated too."

She laughed at that because how he reacted to her then made so much sense now. It was like he dreaded seeing her, which made her even more annoyed.

"Should I come here before your shift starts then?" he asked.

Yasmin noticed the flutter in her stomach at what that meant. He wanted to keep seeing her, and she would like that very much. If he kept this up, she would be in deep trouble of falling in love with him, which was not an unwelcome idea.

There were so many things about him that she liked now, traits she couldn't possibly see if she decided to only hate him.

"What's your schedule like?"

"Hmm," he looked up at the ceiling as if his calendar of activities were there to review. "I have a trip next week."

"Well then, that's ok. My shift might be back to normal non-zombie hours when you return."

"Can we have sex in the hospital?"

"Kota," she hit his arm playfully.

"I'm just curious." He laughed.

"It's like me asking you if we can have sex on stage."

"No," Kota answered, too fast. "Too many people."

"It's the same thing. It's my place of work."

"Can't let too many people see you." He playfully bit her shoulder.

"Why, 'cause you're embarrassed?"

"No." Kota looked at her, "No, not like that. Can't let many people see you, 'cause you're mine, that's what I meant. No."

She laughed at his panic and watched his eyes widen at that thought.

"I'm a little selfish with the things I own," he added.

"So you *own* me now?"

He covered his face, "Ah, shit. That's not what I meant. I'm shutting up now."

Yasmin laughed, letting her hand settle on his nape as his ears turned pink from embarrassment. "I'm just teasing you."

"You like doing that."

"Do you hate it?"

"No," Kota smiled. "It's great foreplay."

"So I shouldn't be stroking your dick anymore?"

"Yasmin," he swung her legs and laid her back down on the couch. He settled on top of her, his weight slowly crashing on her body. "Can I ask you something sex-related?"

"Sure."

"If you have fantasies, you'll tell me, right?"

She laughed. "Why? Are you going to do them?"

"Yeah." He was dead serious too, which made her laugh even more. "I'm not kidding."

He had been so gentle, so loving with her these last four nights — except for his bursts of impatience with biting her in places and growling into her neck — but Yasmin often wondered what it would be like to have him lose all his control.

She pulled him closer to whisper in his ear. He listened, took a moment, then looked back at her. "Really?"

She nodded.

"Give me a safe word."

"That's going overboard. I said *a little*. Just spank me *a little*."

Kota smiled, "I know, but it's better to have one still. I'm a newbie here."

The warmth in her core tuned into goo, her heart some-where turning into a puddle, too. *A safe word.* She wanted to say his name because it was starting to look like he was the safest place she had right now.

"Orange," she said, and the smile that he gave her made her toes curl.

"Orange." He echoed and kissed her on her lips, completely melting her insides.

———

He left early that morning, woke her up gently to tell her he had to go, and all she could do was nod and fall asleep right after.

Yasmin prepared herself for work and made her way down the stairs when she ran into Mary, the President of the Home Associations Board. They were acquainted, of course, she was the person she ran to that day Kota woke her up with his voice.

"Ms. Guerra, what are you doing using the stairs?" Mary asked but then remembered. "Oh yes, unfortunate situation. I heard you and Mr. Dizon got stuck in the elevator last week. Of all the people, huh?"

She laughed nervously.

"He hasn't been making a noise since, has he?"

Well, Yasmin tilted her head at the memory of Kota, who howled during his release last night, but that was a different matter. "No. He's been very respectful."

He was, that was true. Sure, she might have some soreness on her bum (which he lovingly tended to after sex), but she allowed that. He was rough but still so gentle, in the way that she knew that he was taking care of her. Her pleasure seemed to be Kota's priority, something Yasmin knew was a rare trait to find in someone she was sharing her bed with.

She realized that she was probably blushing and cleared her throat. "I think we can lift the No Noise Policy for him now."

Mary laughed. "I'm sure he doesn't mind anymore, Ms. Guerra. There are only a few days left."

She was right. His punishment was ending soon, and it didn't matter to both of them. She is *so*...smitten with him now and learned to appreciate the things that made him *him.* Even her cat started hanging around him more, watching him cook, asking him for kibble, and waiting for him by the door.

And she loved that, loved hearing his voice through the door, through the stairs—it was becoming the sound of her home.

"It's sad to see them go, but *well.* On to bigger things for them." Mary continued.

Yasmin opened her mouth in confusion.

"They're moving to that new condo. We can't compete

with a high-rise condo. We're a modest apartment building, pretty good community…"

"They're moving?" she repeated.

"Yes, darling," Mary waved her hand as if she was telling her to catch up quickly. "All of them. I bet they're already packed. There are only a few days left."

nine

. . .

THEY TOOK them to the new apartments and he couldn't lie, having more space *is* awesome. Even more awesome? There were only two bedrooms. Two beds.

"How do you feel about this?" He asked Chili.

Chili rubbed his eyes as he looked at the window's skyline view. He simply nodded.

"Which room is yours?" Kota asked. "Rock, paper, scissors?"

"Sure," Chili shrugged, poising his hand for the game. "If I win, I get the bigger room."

The bigger room was what he wanted to get, not because it was bigger, but because it had a view. Yasmin's room also had a view, so he thought that she would prefer that. *If* she ever wanted to go there.

Chili tapped his head. "Stop imagining your lady over there. It's my room."

Kota playfully punched his arm. "Stop imagining me imagining her."

"We can't bring girls here, company policy."

"I know." He nodded.

They played best out of three, and Chili won the bigger

room. He did a quick dance and disappeared to yell his victories to his new room.

Kota checked the other room and decided that it wasn't so bad. It was, still, his own space. Without a double deck. Just a nice, queen-sized bed.

Could fit Yasmin. He wasn't allowed to, but *still*.

He blushed at that thought of last night. It was painful for him to tear himself away from her bed that morning, especially since it felt like they'd established something new and deeper with what transpired. There's a certain level of trust that she shared with him, and he recognized that.

He still couldn't believe how the last few nights have been, but he wouldn't dare question it. Kota was riding the wave, so to speak. He would ride the wave for however long he could. The last few days were simply the perfect fit, and he realized that it was what he had been missing. He was all work that even with play, he still found himself worrying about it. It was hard not to worry about his job and his future, but with Yasmin, he was present. It's all he ever needed to be.

Kota closed the door to his would-be room and called over to his new roommate. "Let's go. I wanna go home early."

———

He couldn't wait to get home to her, but it had been a full day of meetings and logistics as they were flying off to LA the next week. He had only a few days left and he wanted to use that all up with her, while they still had this nice momentum.

Kota was sure the tour would be hard for him, with him developing this craving every night. He was like Pavlov's dog, every time it reached the evening, he would just go seek her, and the longer it took, the crankier he gets.

"Put this man out of his misery," Oli joked as he pointed to him.

Kota laughed, knowing that they were all just teasing him.

It was hard to hide these things from the boys, especially when he hasn't been sleeping in his bed for the last few days. He would appear in the morning, and most of them would be awake by then.

He was relieved to find out that nobody actually really needed him to wake them up. They were all grown boys who could make it to their schedules, even Yuan.

Sam wrapped up the meeting, and they all rode the company shuttle that took them home. He changed first and ate some dinner with the boys before running up to her apartment.

Kota knocked on her door with a light tap and heard her unlock it.

He smiled as soon as he saw her. "Did you wait long?"

She grabbed his hand and pulled him in, closing the door with her other hand. She locked the door and then tiptoed to kiss him.

He kissed her back and grabbed the back of her head to cradle.

"Fuck me here," she said.

"What?"

She pulled him down.

"The kitchen floor?"

"Shh." Yasmin kissed him again, pulling his hips down to hers. "Just do it quick."

Kota grinned. "Aren't you romantic?"

She grabbed on his pants but he held her hand to stop her from fumbling.

"I'll do it," he said, calming her down. He didn't know *why* she was suddenly like this—not that he was complaining—but he didn't want them having sex to feel rash. He always put a lot of thought into being with her. He made sure to please her first and to understand what her body wanted.

His hand snaked into her pants, fingers running into her

slit. She arched at that first touch, and he watched her face turn up. She swallowed a breath and relaxed under his hand as he settled in.

"I want to touch you," She insisted. She didn't need to ask again. He let her hand cup him. The friction of her hand rubbing through his pants made the hair on the back of his neck stand up. She unbuttoned his pants and pulled the zipper down, and he felt himself spring forward the moment her fingers curled around his shaft. He let out a groan and muffled a curse.

She kissed him softly, content that they were touching each other. Her body started to move to the rhythm as his finger worked her clit. They looked at each other, watched every gasp and shudder until he entered one finger inside of her. She closed her eyes and held his arm as he curled it up, preparing her for the next digit.

"Yes, *please.*" She shifted her hips, and he knew he hit the spot when she moaned. He kissed that off of her as if claiming his reward. She was wet and sticky in his hands, and he knew that he was ready for her too. He took his hands off of her for a regrettable moment to pull the rest of her pants down when he noticed something at the tip of his fingers.

Blood.

Kota scanned Yasmin's face, then ran a hand through her sex, "Yasmin."

"Huh?"

He bent down and ran a hand over her again, worried that he hurt her. "Are you hurt?"

"No," she lifted her head.

Kota looked at the blood on his finger, "Are you getting your period?"

She scrambled then, shut her legs, and pulled her clothing from the floor and onto the bathroom. He followed her then, aware that he was still aroused, but washed his hands on the faucet and waited for her outside of the bathroom.

"Do you want me to get anything?" He offered.

"No," she said through the door. "You can go."

He frowned at that. She wants him to go? After that? "Yasmin, it's okay."

There was no response from her end, and by the time she got out, she simply walked past him.

"I can get you stuff downstairs."

"Kota, just go," she said with an exasperated sigh. "We're not gonna have sex."

"Um?"

"*Anymore*," she added. "Please go."

"I don't see what the big deal is, you got your period. What's the problem?"

"You got what you came here for, didn't you?" Yasmin asked.

"Not really," he looked down his pants.

"Next time, yeah?" she continued to walk off like it was no big deal.

"What are you talking about?" Kota stepped back. "I don't come up here just for sex."

She looked at him with a raised brow. "Then what do *you* come here for? Couldn't be for my pleasing personality."

He couldn't help but laugh, despite knowing that she might find that annoying. He really does come up to her for *this*. Her. Her humor. Her snark. Her wit. On top of all the things that made him practically addicted to her by now.

He liked her so much, he just couldn't imagine not running over to see her every night.

"How did you know?" He asked.

Yasmin walked over to the couch. "Go home, I'm gonna be in pain in the next few hours. See you next week."

Kota followed her though, and he did remember how she likened him to a dog.

She raised a hand to his chest. "I'm not kidding."

"Why? I'm not afraid of blood."

"I'm going to cry."

"That's cool, do you want ice cream with that?" He asked.

She paused, and he smiled at how she considered it, knew that he gave her an offer she couldn't refuse. "Do you want me to order food?"

"I want meat."

"Quarter pounders sound good right now."

"Alright, who is she?" she asked suddenly. He gave her a confused look. "Who taught you these things? Why are you suddenly the menstruation whisperer?"

Kota laughed, but she remained confused, and a bit cranky.

She whispered, "You don't have a girlfriend, do you?"

"Jesus, Yasmin." He waved her off. "I'm not cheating on anyone with you. Sit down, and let me order you food."

She did what he said and watched him order their food. She asked for large fries and a large Coke too.

"I just think we skipped a lot of things," Yasmin suddenly said.

"Like what?"

"Like did you even consider asking me if I have a boyfriend?"

Kota frowned. "Do you?"

"No," she answered. "But I could have a boyfriend. People do that, you know. Sleep with someone else even when they're with others."

He simply nodded, being on the other side of that fence. It was a hard pill to swallow.

"If I had a boyfriend, what would you do?"

"Right now? Cancel your order." That was the first thing, but he didn't want to think of it further. It would ruin *so many* things, and he was happy with how things are unfolding.

"That *would* hurt me."

"Why were you trying to have sex with me there?" he asked.

"Oh," she blushed. "I don't know if you know this, but menstruation can make you super horny. But I also didn't know I'm having it like, right now. I thought at least in the morning. So I'm like trying to catch that window."

He smiled at that, relieved to find out that he wasn't the only one trying to squeeze things in, knowing full well things are bound to happen, and they are just both desperate to keep this bubble they'd been in.

"Anyway, I'm already late for like a couple of days. Don't panic. I think it's just from all the sex I've been having lately. I think my uterus is confused from all the action."

He laughed, but he was aware that he was blushing too. Her saying "Don't panic" was really cute. He would be panicking more if they weren't being safe, but they agreed to be responsible from Day 1. His cheeks felt warm, and his stomach felt…funny. In a good way.

"And we only have a few days before your trip, and by then, I'll be reunited with my celibacy."

"Same. We can have sex in the shower." He didn't dwell on it too much, but he noted that she considered his time being away as being celibate. It was the same case for him— work and touring haven't always been the ideal time for hooking up, contrary to what others think. *If you wanted an organized tour, don't do any relations.* No relationships or situationships are the company's preference, but they know that would be near impossible. It was easier though, to not have any relations at all, and he has been riding on that for more than a year.

"How are you single?" she leaned in, eyes narrowed in disbelief. "Don't you have people just volunteering for that?"

He let out a snort, flattered that she was asking him this. "I didn't have hot neighbors before."

He was single because there was no time to date. There

was not enough time to build something and having her upstairs possibly played a role in making it a little more convenient for him. *She* wasn't convenient though, she was quite possibly one of the most inconvenient people he's ever met, and yet…he liked her. Of all the people, he liked her.

She pouted. "You only date your neighbors?"

"No, I'm saying *you're* hot."

"Stop hitting on me." She wrinkled her nose, and he pinched it in response. "I already slept with you."

"Yes, but see, I want to *keep* sleeping with you."

"When are you going to tell me that you're moving?" She suddenly asked.

"Tonight?"

"How convenient."

"I just saw the new apartment today," he explained. "So I really didn't know if it was happening. But today, yeah, I guess it's happening. We signed the contract."

Yasmin nodded. He thought that there was a question begging to be asked next, but she didn't say anything anymore. They waited for their burgers to come, and ate them in front of the television with the cat asking for pieces of the patty.

They slept together that night, with her hogging the pillows for her lower back and hips. It would be a good idea for him to leave her all to herself so she could move all she wanted, but she told him to stay, and that was all he needed to hear.

ten

. . .

A COUPLE of things they accomplished before he went off to his little work trip, aka an overseas concert: 1) They exchanged numbers; 2) They had shower sex.

It was ridiculous to think she had been sleeping with someone who didn't have her number, but then again, he knew where she lived. That's just one of the things that didn't follow the norm when it came to her relationship with Kota.

When he left that day, he mentioned that it was going to be hectic, and she took that as *don't text him*.

Which was fine -- they were not in a relationship. They were sleeping together, consensually, with a non-spoken understanding that they were just sleeping together. If they were getting into a relationship then there would have been invitations to go outside, go on a real date, and all that.

But looking at the past behavior, Yasmin understood that she was some sort of a booty call, without the actual call. He was just knocking on her door every night because it was convenient, even when he said he wasn't coming up just for sex.

That was cute, but she had a feeling that the moment he moved, there would be less knocking, and her life would resume. Sexless, and noiseless, but hey, she preferred that a couple of days ago.

She treated his little work trip as her training for the day he moved out and completely disappeared from her life.

————

Kota stared at his phone, frowned, and checked the signal, the internet, his battery??? There were five messages on his end and no messages on the other.

Did she give him a fake number?

No. He made her phone ring the time she gave her number so she could save his.

Did she not save his number?

But he already said, *hey, this is Kota.*

He lifted his chin and stared at the ceiling, feeling the swipe of the brush under his lids.

"Reception's bad," Steph, their makeup artist, said softly, kind of sweetly, as if she was trying to soothe him from an upcoming tantrum. "Did you even get roaming on?"

He smiled. It was so hard to keep anything from people. They worked so closely that stuff like these gets noticed. It's also how things leaked, even if they learned to trust the people around them.

Steph ran a hand on his lid. "Don't stress."

"Do I look stressed?" He was aware he sounded a bit defensive.

She moved back, looking at her work from a certain distance before moving back in to refine his eye makeup.

"Relax your brows, Kota," she said instead.

He took a deep breath and decided not to think about it. It's just that he was worried his messages weren't getting through. He was also worried that she didn't like getting texts and that he should just get *the* message: she doesn't like him that way.

She liked him *some* type of way, but maybe she preferred not getting the updates, or just getting to know him.

Kota wanted to curl into his seat but knew Steph was working on making his eyes symmetrical so he didn't.

So much about not thinking about it.

Wasn't this his rule? He was decidedly single for a while because he didn't want this. He was happy focusing on his job and could always worry about having someone later.

She was right, he did have people volunteering to be his girlfriend—if he wanted to have one, he could, and it would probably be less stressful than this. She didn't want to be his girlfriend, at least that's what it seemed.

Steph placed a hand on his cheek and it reminded him of her, how she liked touching the apple of his cheek and that made him scowl.

"Alright, do you want to talk about it?" Step sighed. She put her brush down as if she's given up on him.

"No," he answered. He looked at his reflection and knew that she wasn't done with her work.

"Just give me the gist," She insisted. "I'll tell you what you need to hear."

Kota considered, but how does he talk about something he hasn't been talking about to anyone anyway? It's not like he's denying being involved with someone, people can see. And people have seen how it's been different for him in the past few days.

"It's not that easy," he said.

"Not all things are, but is it worth it?"

"Huh?"

Steph smiled, "Just throwing out random daily inspo shit at you. Not everything is easy, but not everything will be hard."

Kota laughed.

"See, you just need a Pinterest board of quotes." Steph picked up her brush. "What else do you need?"

A text back. Yasmin to like him back. Yasmin, really, just Yasmin.

"No answer is also an answer," she added.

And she was right. She would tell him what he needed to hear.

———

She couldn't blame her period anymore but Yasmin just felt awful. The entire time. Her being annoyed at her feeling awful was not helping, too. She spent the last days locked up in her apartment.

She had a day off and didn't do her usual errands which made her friend Nico worry. It's why she was there, in front of her fridge, stocking it up with food.

Yasmin stood from the distance, watching her friend while she kept herself possibly hidden in this big cozy hoodie Kota left on her couch the other day.

Nico flashed the big chocolate bars at her. "Emergency stash."

"Thanks."

Even the chocolates didn't look good, what the hell was happening to her?

Sex withdrawal, that was it. She had good sex for a week straight and now her body's been rejecting the sudden absence.

But it wasn't even just the sex, it was...

She tried to come up with the proper term for it, but all she was getting was this sinking feeling in her stomach.

You miss him.

His last update to her was last night, and she had refrained from replying to him because...

His texts weren't exactly texts to respond to. It felt like she was reading from a feed. It was updates. And she had no updates for him, except that she'd finished a K-Drama series since he'd been away. She sat through it in one day.

"How's everything?" Nico asked.

Yasmin's brows rose.

"Must be quiet for you these days, your hot neighbors are away."

Right. Nico is probably more updated than her by now.

"Oh. That's why you weren't complaining about why you didn't see any of them today."

"Concert looked good," Nico continued. "We should watch them."

She rejected that idea. *Too weird*. Not because she wouldn't enjoy their music or performance, but it would be weird to see Kota that way. It would further show her how unattainable he was, and how the last few days were just a drop in a bucket of luck.

She hasn't won the lottery, but the Universe decided, *this* is your stroke of luck.

But even in that, Yasmin scowled, because he wasn't supposed to be unattainable. He was human too. She's seen that—him—closely, and had her arms around him, understood his desire. There's so much that is close for her to reach if she actually took it.

She *knew* this, but there are parts of her brain that seemed to disagree and would like to separate Kota from the person she was with.

It wasn't his fault but also…it would help a lot he assured her.

Then again, he wasn't here, and how could she say so?

And does she even have the right to ask for it?

Nico looked at her phone screen and laughed. "They're shopping."

"How are you this updated with their lives?" Yasmin asked, although she really didn't want to know the answer.

"They have a group chat feature with their fans, duh," Nico answered. "It's exclusive to members."

"And do they just leave you all little updates about their day?"

"I guess. Like how boyfriends do," Her friend stuck her tongue out. "They have their ways of updating though. Sam likes to post his meal."

"Yuan likes to message at midnight, often with random thoughts." Nico went on.

"Oh, he's *that* guy."

"He's so single."

Yasmin snorted.

"Kota updates with selfies. Just a general reporting of him being present in so and so."

She rolled her eyes with *selfies*. Thank God she didn't get those with her updates. All she got was him trying to start a conversation. And she didn't get those in time, anyway. She would get them at odd hours, sometimes while she was at work, or while asleep, and...she's aware that these are all excuses. She could reply to him any time, but did she want to?

She was reminded of the time he asked for her name, and how telling him that meant she was opening the door for him. She didn't think much of it when he asked for her number before he left, she was secure in the post-sex haze, and truthfully, everything seemed fine with him around.

It's when he was away that she started to think otherwise, and that seemed to be a *her* problem than his problem.

"He hasn't been updating though." she heard Nico say.

"He hasn't?" her head lifted.

"They're not required to, but when they're on the road, each member usually uploads something. That's ok, he has fan cams from the concert anyway."

"How is he?" she asked, and she was aware of how that

sounded. Like she was inquiring about *him.* Like he was a person she cared about.

Nico caught that, because she is her friend, and may know more than she leads on. "He looks fine."

Yasmin nodded, shrugged that off and walked over to turn on her TV.

"Are you okay?" Nico asked. "Your funk seemed to last longer this month. What's going on?"

"I think I caught a bug." She faked a cough.

"Is the bug called 'feelings'?"

Her friend gave her a smirk, and she didn't know if she should laugh it off or vehemently deny it.

"You're not that hard to read, Yasmin." Nico mused. "You don't think I notice these things? You had a nice glow around you the last time I was here. Now, you look like shit. No offense."

"I feel like shit."

"Aw, sorry, babe." Nico stroked her hair. "Plus, I recognized that hoodie from a mile away."

She looked down at the clothing and then blushed.

"I told you your boyfriend posts selfies." Nico stuck her tongue out.

"Boyfriend," she sputtered. "That's not…"

"I see. You're in that weird spot. That sucks." Her friend frowned. "Well, this is exactly why I only subscribe to LuvByte's group chat. I get all the perks without committing. They get the money and the subscription. I can unsubscribe anytime I want. It's a win-win situation. Capitalism wins."

Yasmin laughed.

Nico sighed, "You can unsubscribe too, you know. The question is, do you want to?"

eleven

. . .

THEY WERE ALREADY in the airport, on their way back home when he first got a reply.

How long?

He reread the texts he sent above to get the context, but he couldn't connect it to anything he said.

How long what?

Til you're back?

Kota felt a burst in his chest the moment he read it like everything else around him exploded into colors. He stood in place for a moment, stared at his phone, and looked up to see Oli give him a weird look.

He ignored him and carried on like everything was normal.

Flying back in a bit

> Are you okay? Didn't hear from you since I
> left.

I don't like texting.

> Call?

I hate calls. Please don't call me unless
you're dying.

He laughed at that, and could almost imagine her telling him that in person. He looked for a quiet corner and pressed the voice text option.

"So how do you want me to communicate, morse code? Smoke signals? Also, this isn't a call, not technically. I am not dying." He sent that over to her.

They were in the lounge area now, and the rest of the boys have been ordering coffee from the nearby Starbucks.

It's the yelling child in the background for me

He thought he walked far enough, but a child was having a tantrum when he recorded that.

> Talk about this when I'm home?

Yes, come up.

> Okay, text you when we're boarding.

I liked the voice message. Kinda miss your
voice.

He smiled at that and recorded his response. "Should I record a wake-up call for you? I can sing that song you hated."

No, don't. I hate you

Just say that you missed me

He typed that, feeling bold.

He was sure he looked like a kid who got the first item on his Christmas checklist when he read her reply.

I already did, didn't I?

———

Despite her saying she didn't like texts, they continued to talk before he had to turn his connection off upon take off. When he landed hours (almost a day) later, he got her texts and replied to them all.

So much for not liking texts, Kota thought. He knew there was more to it than that.

By the time they arrived at Roman's Court, they were all hungry, sleepy, and in need of a shower. There were 6 other boys in line for the bathroom, but half of them decided they will sleep first instead, and the rest were keen on getting food first.

Kota wanted the shower, the bed, and the girl upstairs.

She would still be at work though, with her shift back to normal hours. He could go to her later.

So he took that shower, ate, and decided to lie down until it was time to see Yasmin. That was the plan anyway—but he fell asleep and didn't wake up until the next day.

———

Kota didn't come up that night as she was expecting, but she had to take into account that the boy had been traveling for hours, after performing for thousands of people.

Of course, he couldn't just go to her.

Did she like it? No. But does she understand it? Sadly, yes.

And also she just had to keep reminding herself that she did not have the right to demand so much time from him.

That was the good thing about their earlier set-up. Coming over was very much *his* choice, and her accepting him was hers.

It was a pretty easy setup then. She thought she'd be able to stretch their time together longer, but since finding out that Kota and the boys were moving, she couldn't help but hear the *tic tic tic* of the clock.

Yasmin knew she had no choice anyway.

She was getting ready for work when she heard a knock. She hated how she jolted out of her seat and ran to her door.

It was Kota, and he came up to her with his hair still sticking up, eyes still puffy. She leaned in to gauge if he was sleepwalking, but he dropped his head to her shoulders instead, in an attempt at a hug.

Yasmin ran a hand over his back, feeling the weight of his body transferring over to her. "Are you awake?"

"Kind of," he said as he wrapped his hands around her.

She felt like his anchor now, and she dragged him inside. Thankfully, he straightened and walked over to her couch where Cosmo welcomed him with generous rubs on his shin. He bent down to pet her cat.

Not my cat getting first dibs, she thought. She shooed Cosmo away, giving him a look. *Mine. My man.*

Kota curled into her sofa, and he looked so tiny at that moment that she didn't know whether to laugh or be touched by it.

This is the Kota she knew, and not the celebrity the other part of her brain had been building up.

"You didn't have to come up if you needed to sleep more."

"I have to pack," he said. "Later. Pack and then move."

"Already?"

He nodded with a yawn. "Wanted to see you last night."

She sat in front of him and watched him speak with his eyes closed. "I have to go to work."

He nodded slowly like he was already drifting off.

She touched the tip of his nose, and he wrinkled it in response.

"I can let you sleep here, just lock my door when you leave."

"Need to talk." He mumbled.

"Yeah, but you're barely awake." She laughed. *This poor guy*. He was trying so hard, and she recognized his effort.

Kota opened his eyes slowly. "Do you have to go now?"

"I have a couple of minutes."

"Why weren't you texting me at first?" he asked.

She smiled. *Of course, he's gonna ask her right away.* "You said it's gonna be hectic."

"But I was texting you."

"I know." She sighed. "I guess I was trying not to make texting a thing between us."

His brows met, and even with his sleepy lids, he looked slightly annoyed. "Because?"

"Because do we want to make this even more complicated?"

That seemed to have waken him up. He lifted his head and used his hand to cradle his chin. "What do you mean?"

"If you're just sleeping with me, should you be updating me with all these things? I'm fine with you just knocking on my door when you need to."

He looked at her like that was such a ridiculous idea. "I told you I wasn't coming up here just for sex."

"You say that now—"

"I'm saying it because I mean it," he cut her off. "I really like you, in case that wasn't obvious from all the sex we're having."

"Sex could be just sex," she countered.

Kota pulled her gently to give her a soft kiss. It was soft enough to be a whisper, but strong enough to say what he wanted to say.

"You should have said that instead," Yasmin said lamely.

"I thought I did." His brows furrowed. "Words of affirmation, that's what you need, yeah?"

"Well, I need all of it." She looked away, embarrassed at what that implied. But words are not enough, words are great and supplementary, but she needed the whole shebang. She needed the time, the physical affection, and the words.

He laughed, "Okay. Do you want to go out this weekend?"

Yasmin leaned back. "This is an option?"

He was laughing still, like everything that she was saying was ridiculous.

"You never asked me out," she defended.

"It's what I'm doing now." Kota ran a hand over her head like she was his pet.

"I'll think about it."

He laid back down on her sofa, smiling at the ceiling. "Okay. I can wait."

She put her hand on his chest. "I have to go."

"I'll walk you down."

"No, you look like you'll fall asleep anytime soon. If you break your neck, your fans will never let me live."

"I'm leaving today."

"I'm seeing you on the weekend anyway."

Kota paused, then smiled. "You're gonna keep doing this to me, aren't you?"

"What?"

"Drive me crazy."

Yasmin smiled, and leaned down to run her hand over his cheek. It always made him smile, which rewarded her with that whisker dimple she always wanted to see.

"You do the same thing to me anyway." She kissed the tip of his nose first, then his lips. "Quits lang tayo."

— THE END —

epilogue

. . .

I LOVE HIM, *I love him, I love him.*

Yasmin leaned her chin on Kota's shoulders, looking over his phone as he scrolled through a gallery of pets up for adoption.

Yasmin always wanted to adopt another cat, and she witnessed how Kota and Cosmo started to bond. She didn't know who charmed whom, but they seemed to get along better. Sometimes, Cosmo snuggles up to Kota more than her, but she doesn't mind.

She loved Kota now, but he didn't know. She hasn't told him yet—not that it would shock him if she finally said it, everything that had been happening between them was building up to this.

He told her he loved her first. It was around the fourth or fifth month since they officially decided to see each other, and he did it so casually, she almost resented how he did it so well. He said it in the morning, upon waking up like it was his first thought.

Yasmin was barely awake then to form a response, but he has been saying it to her since, like a constant reminder to her before he leaves for work, in random voice messages he sends her when he's overseas (apart from the songs he records on his phone for her to sleep to like he was her lullaby generator), whenever she gets the urge to ask him, *but why do you love me? Elaborate.*

Kota humors her with these things, and plays with her a lot, which she loves about him. He knew how to take care of her and to keep her entertained.

"Ah wait, let me show you that trick," Kota turned to her, switching to his phone gallery. They were in an elevator, leading up to his new apartment. "I taught Cosmo something."

He clicked the video to play. "Watch."

In the video, Kota was holding Cosmo as he started to sing one of his songs, only to let the cat finish the last syllable of every line with a soft *meow*. The cat was meowing in tune, and it was hilarious to watch them both look into each other's eyes like they were performing this for her.

"Oh my god, he's a singer." Yasmin wiped a tear from her eye after laughing so much.

The elevator door opened just in time for him to slide the phone back into his pocket. They stepped out, heading towards his unit.

"How long did you guys do that?"

"Why, do you want to do it too?" He teased. They were going to pick up Cosmo who spent a weekend at Kota's while Yasmin went home to see her parents. It was his first time caring for the cat without her, and it looked like it went well.

They stopped at the door with Kota saying, "I should tell you that he loves it here."

She narrowed her eyes, "I know I'm thinking of adopting, but that doesn't mean I don't want my cat back."

He laughed, "That's not what I meant."

She leaned back to let him explain.

"I make a good cat Dad," Kota announced.

"I agree." She answered. Kota had claimed some kind of

ownership with Cosmo. He started sharing the cat's pictures to the fan group chat, much to his fans' delight and interest. He did this with her consent, of course, and kept her identity as the owner private.

"Really?" He suddenly looked relieved, one hand still at the door knob.

Yasmin smiled. "Oh, I'm sorry, did I not ask you yet? Do you want to adopt a cat with me?"

His eyes widened, "Seriously?"

She nodded. She thought he already knew what she meant when she brought up the adoption but seeing him worked up over it was really cute too.

"I get to be an official cat dad? With papers and everything?" Kota asked.

"Yeah, we can sign the papers."

Kota smiled widely, then opened the door. Their new unit was a quiet space. There are plush seats in the living room but her eyes went straight to the black cat sleeping on top of a pillow.

Yasmin rushed to Cosmo, softly petting his head while he continued to sleep.

"Stay for a bit."

"I thought that wasn't allowed," She said.

Kota shrugged, "Eh, what are they gonna do?"

They did just renew their contract after some negotiation. That's given Kota a lot of confidence these past few days.

"Where's Chili?" Yasmin asked, craning her neck towards his roommate's room.

"Studio." He answered, going to the fridge. "He's working on a solo, so he's been sleeping there sometimes."

"So you're here alone?"

Kota closed the fridge door. "Yeah, we can't sleep over here. They'll fine me."

"Assuming mo." She stuck her tongue out.

He laughed, handing her a glass of water. "I can sleep over at your place tonight, right?"

Yasmin felt silly for assuming he would because honestly, when has he not? The man comes home to her whenever he can. "I don't know. I feel pretty tired."

He frowned. "Yasmin, I haven't seen you in three days, *please*, I just want a cuddle."

She laughed at him because he was so easy to tease. She kissed the tip of his nose, which he wriggled. She patted his cheek and told him she was just kidding. She also needed a cuddle. They've gone through longer times without seeing each other, especially when their jobs were making it difficult for them, but as far as she's concerned, a day or a week doesn't make much difference. She missed him all the time.

"Let's look at the cats again." She suggested. She's been visiting the adoption site for a while now and has grown the habit of looking at the pets' photos.

They settled on the couch, with her putting her legs over his, looking over at her phone to scroll through photos of cats and their quick bios.

"It's like Tinder for cats." Kota looked over as she *awwed* at every cat.

"And what do you know about Tinder, hmm?"

"Nothing, Goddess." He sighed with a hint of teasing.

"We can schedule a day to meet them in person."

"Let's do it before the promo so I can still help you get stuff sorted," he said. LuvByte has only released one EP since they got together but is now in the works of releasing an album. His days will get more hectic leading up to this.

"I can take my pawternity leave without questions."

Yasmin laughed. "You're taking this way too seriously."

She continued to scroll through, waiting for the extra pinch in her heart. Every cat is cute, but Yasmin thought she would know if it was the right one.

"Wait." His hand hovered over hers, and she scrolled back up to a photo of a ginger cat with a pink nose.

Yasmin looked at him.

"It's an orange cat," he said excitedly.

She looked at the cat, then back at him.

"It's Kota, Jr. With orange hair, get it?"

I love him, I love him, I love him. There it was again, willing itself out of her tongue, like a bird on a cage singing its song.

"Is it a girl?"

"No, it's a boy." She answered.

"He's cute, right?" He held her phone to take a closer look.

Yasmin pulled on his shirt to make him lean in closer. He hasn't colored his hair orange since they first met—his recent makeover has been kinder to his scalp—but she did kinda miss that look on him and wondered how she would feel if he had it back.

Kota put the phone down, aware that her attention has shifted. He flashed her that smile she loved so much, one that told her that he was so ridiculously happy.

"Hey." She ran her thumb over that whisker dimple before kissing him. "I love you."

It didn't matter so much how or when and where she said it. What mattered more was that she was so sure when she did. He kissed her back and didn't say much.

"Kinda expected you to react more when I said that." Yasmin pulled back.

"Hmm?" Kota tilted his head. "Why?"

She rolled her eyes, "It's only the first time I ever said it to you."

He paused and looked at her with furrowed brows.

Yasmin gasped, "It's not?"

"You already told me you love me," Kota told her. "Many times."

"When?"

"In the mornings, when I kiss you goodbye. I tell you I love you, and you say it back. It's more of a murmur but I..." He looked at her incredulously. "Were you not aware of that?"

Well. She has been saying it back to him in her head, or so she thought. Yasmin laughed at herself for making such a big deal out of it. All along, she had already been saying it to him.

"That's hilarious," she giggled. "What else do I tell you in the mornings?"

Kota bit back a smile. "Lots of things. *Don't go. Pogi mo. You're so good. Best sex of my life.*"

"Lies, a bunch of lies."

He gave her a smug look, the same one that she found so annoyingly endearing now. "Are they, though?"

Yasmin playfully covered his face with her hand, laughing with him. "I hate your face so much. I hate you."

He grabbed her hand and kissed her palm. "Yeah, yeah. I love you, too."

acknowledgments

This book will not be complete without the help of these talented, kind, and hardworking people. They've worked with me to better my craft, and the stories I wanted to tell, and in helping me attain my vision for this series.

My editing team: Layla and KB, Rix (for the earlier ones!)

My cover team: Reg and Melon Illustrations

My emotional support pets: Shira, Shadow, and Pepper (who obviously inspired Cosmo's habits).

Family and friends, who cheered me on from Book 1 to Book…*what number are we in now?* Thank you for filling me up with the good stuff.

#romanceclass for the continuous inspiration (and the prompts!).

My readers who have given this one a try - whether it's your first or nth book from me, thank you for enjoying my books.

bonus content

Songs I listened to while writing and editing "Orange" aka my unsolicited music recommendation:

- I Miss When I Smelled Like You by girlpuppy
- Hamilton by Hazel English
- Slow Dancing (Hazel English Remix) by Aly & AJ, Hazel English
- Youth by KIHYUN
- Okay Okay I'm Wrong I'm Sorry by Ourselves the Elves
- obsessed by thuy
- Clementine by Wet
- Crowded Room by Selena Gomez feat. 6LACK
- Poetry by Devin Kennedy
- What If I Love You by Gatlin
- Always by Babygirl
- Easily by Bruno Major
- wish that i could by UMI
- FOOL 4 U by MICHELLE
- Deny by MONSTA X

also by dawn lanuza

From the LuvByte Series:

Five Stars

Noted

- The Boyfriend Backtrack
- What About Today
- The Hometown Hazard
- Break-up Anniversary
- Stay A Little Longer
- In the City of Angels

Poetry:

- The Last Time I'll Write About You
- This is How it Starts
- You Are Here
- I Must Belong Somewhere
- I Miss My Friends: An Illustrated Poem

about the author

Dawn Lanuza writes contemporary romance, young adult fiction, and poetry.

She started to self-publish in 2014 with her debut romance novel, The Boyfriend Backtrack, which was eventually published by Anvil Publishing. In 2016, she also self-published her first poetry collection, "The Last Time I'll Write About You" which debuted at #1 on Amazon's Hot New Releases and stayed on its Bestsellers chart for over a year before it was re-released into an expanded and revised edition by Andrews McMeel Publishing.

She's been choosing her favorite member in every boyband as a child raised by MTV. She loves music, pop stars, and creating imaginary scenarios with them.

www.ingramcontent.com/pod-product-compliance
Lightning Source LLC
Chambersburg PA
CBHW031450150726
47990CB00007B/2690